The Ki. g g

Rosemary Hayes

First published in 2025 by Sharpe Books.

Chapter One

November 1808

Will Fraser sat slumped in the corner of the stagecoach. The skid was on as the vehicle slowly made its way, creaking and groaning, down the long hill into the city of Durham. Will was bone weary, his clothes travel stained and his body aching from the constant lurching of the coach. He had hardly slept during the long journey from London and now, as he stared out at the grand old cathedral rising up from the rocks and woods around it, he felt sick with dread.

It was late afternoon and already the westering sun of early November was sinking fast. He could not travel further today. The coach would stop here at the Three Tuns Inn in Durham to change horses and he would be obliged to spend the night at the inn, then find a nag to hire and ride out the next morning to his father's farm.

How can I face them?

In the space of a month, his life had been ruined. Betrayed and falsely accused, he had been discharged from the army in disgrace and without a pension. No longer a Captain, Will had returned from the war in Portugal with his friend and wounded colleague, Sergeant Armstrong.

It had been a miserable journey, first on a hospital ship, tossed about in the Bay of Biscay and then, after disembarking at Spithead, transferring onto a Thames barge which took them to London.

In London, Will had sought out his brother, Jack, only to find that Jack had disappeared and then, when Will could not conceive that his own circumstances could be made any worse, an even greater tragedy had occurred.

Will reflected on all that had happened during the last ten days and wondered whether he could have acted differently. Yet again his thoughts went back to that fateful event on the French coast.

He was jerked from his dismal reverie as the coach shuddered to a halt outside the inn. He heaved himself out, shouldered his

1

haversack and entered The Three Tuns.

It took a while to arrange for the hire of a horse for the morrow and a room for the night and to order food, and by the time this was settled, the horses had been changed and the mail coach was setting off again for its final destination of Newcastle. Will stood outside the door of the inn for a while and watched as the new team of horses toiled painfully up the steep streets towards Framwellgate Bridge to cross the River Wear. Then he sighed and went inside.

The journey North had been costly and the dinner served at the inn did not come cheap, but the hot roast beef followed by apple tart and accompanied by a few glasses of claret, revived him somewhat. In his room at the top of the building, he sat down at a table and counted out his remaining coin and saw, with relief, that there was plenty to pay for his return journey. Looking at the coins laid out in front of him, he was reminded of how he had come by them, and who had given them to him.

Blood money.

Then he got to his feet and started to pace up and down the wooden floorboards.

How many times has Armstrong said to me that none of this was my fault, that I was used and deceived? Yet I cannot rid myself of the burden of guilt. I cannot forgive myself. If only I had not believed the man. I'm a simple soldier, used to dealing with simple commands, not with half-truths and political intrigue.

At length he stopped his pacing. He sat on the edge of his bed and took off his long boots. They were mud stained and down at heel but there was little point in cleaning them now. The weather tomorrow would, no doubt, still be dank and overcast and they would become even more mud spattered when he rode out to his father's farm.

He stripped off his waistcoat and pantaloons and put them over the chair with his tailcoat. All his clothes were filthy, but he had no others.

Will lay down on the bed, pulled the covers over him and, almost immediately fell into an exhausted sleep.

But his dreams would not let him rest and recent events came back to haunt him. He tossed and turned, shouting out as he heard, again, that fatal gunshot and saw the two graves dug so hastily in the sandy soil on the French coast.

Then the look of hatred on Clara's face when he told her what had happened. The vision was so clear in his dream that it woke him and he sat up and rubbed his eyes. Clara had put her life in jeopardy to keep him informed. She had trusted him.

How cruelly I let her down.

The sun had not risen but Will was fully awake now. He lit a candle, splashed some water on his face from the bowl on the chest by the window, and felt the stubble on his cheeks.

He ran a comb through his hair and allowed himself a brief smile as he remembered the transformation the two young actresses had wrought on his appearance – the dyeing of his hair, the trimming of his eyebrows and the salve to lighten his complexion. They had done an excellent job of it and had made his strong resemblance to his brother even more marked so that he had been able to deceive folk into thinking that he was, indeed, Jack.

If only they had not been so skilled. If only my disguise had not worked so well. If only ...

Then he straightened his shoulders. It was pointless to dwell on what might have been. Now he must be man enough to face the consequences of his actions. He set about brushing down his tailcoat though, in truth, it made little difference and it was still a sorry sight when he had finished.

At least I shall be able to change my clothes when I reach my father's house. Unless he refuses to shelter me when he hears my news.

Dawn was just breaking when he made his way down the stairs to the main room of the inn. The only person up and about was a young maid, yawning as she set about laying the fire. She jumped to her feet when he entered the room and bobbed a brief curtsy.

'What can I get you sir?'

Will stretched. 'A little breakfast, but I am in no hurry.'

The girl wiped her hands on her pinafore. 'I'll go directly to the kitchen.'

'There is no need to hurry,' Will repeated. 'I cannot leave until it is fully light.'

He walked to the window and looked out. Streaks of light were showing in the East but the last of the stars had yet to fade from the sky. The bare trees outside were moving as the wind got up, tearing the last of the leaves from the branches and sending them swirling to the ground which was covered in puddles from overnight rain. He did not relish the long ride to the farm.

He could hear more movement now as the inn came to life. There were low murmurings and some laughter coming from the kitchen and, in due course, the maid reappeared with some bread and porridge for him. Anticipating the reception he would have from his parents, his stomach churned but he forced himself to eat, knowing that his exhausted body needed food to sustain him during his ride.

Having finished his breakfast and settled his account with the innkeeper, Will made his way to the stables at the back of the building. There was a lad waiting for him and a sturdy cob was already saddled. Will inspected the horse with a practised eye, ran his hands down its legs and flanks, adjusted the girth and the length of the stirrup leathers, then turned to the boy.

'He will do me well.'

'He's not the fastest, sir, but he'll go for miles without tiring.'

Will handed the lad a coin and then, his haversack over his shoulders, he swung himself up into the saddle, took up the reins and trotted out into the road.

As he headed West out of the town, the weather worsened and squalls of rain-filled wind battered him so that he was tempted to return to the warmth of the inn and put off his journey. Indeed, at one point, he drew rein and was about to turn back but as he peered ahead, he thought he saw a faint gleam of sun coming through in the far distance, so he pressed his heels into the horse's flanks and plodded on.

The morning wore on and the track became steeper as they headed into the hills. The desolate moorland stretched either side of them, dotted with sheep in sodden huddles sheltering against stone walls. He had loved this moorland country in his youth, but then it seemed always sunlit and welcoming. So different from its grim and threatening mood today.

His father's farm lay on the outskirts of Alston, a remote village in the hollow of the hills and at the confluence of two rivers. It was well into the afternoon by the time Will approached the settlement and as he passed by the entrance to the manor house he halted. He sat astride his horse for some time, beside the stone pillars which flanked the gateway leading onto the drive, and stared up towards the house. It belonged to the landowner - Clara's father. Will's father was one of his tenants.

Has Clara already reached home? Is she telling them what has happened? How I wish she had come with me. We could have told our families together. But she will never look kindly on me again, never trust me.

Will sighed, remembering her last words to him, when he had suggested that they travel North together. He could see her now, her fists clenched, her back to him, staring out of the window of her London rooms, into the yard below. Not even turning round as she spat out the words 'I think not' before summoning her maid to show him out of the door and out of her life.

The light was already fading as Will reached the track which led up to his father's farm on the far side of the village and as the old house came into sight, so achingly familiar, surrounded by barns and outbuildings, he had to fight the urge to stop.

Now, in these last minutes, they still think that all is well. That all is as it should be. And I have to shatter their illusions.

He rode on doggedly, even urging his horse into a trot, anxious now, to get it over with, trying not to imagine their misery as the dreams they had had for their sons were crushed.

When he reached the farmhouse, he slid stiffly from the saddle and stood at the door, unsure whether to stable the horse first. But then the decision was taken from him and there was a shout from inside.

His mother had seen him.

The door was flung open and then she was there, a little greyer, a little stouter, but with a wide smile on her face and her arms outstretched.

'My dear boy,' she said, taking his face in her hands. And then, stepping back a little, laughing. 'Why for a moment I thought it was Jack, your resemblance is stronger than ever, but now I see that it is you, Will. Oh thank God you are returned to us.'

She turned in the doorway and shouted into the hall behind. 'Come quickly Father, it is our brave soldier son.'

She was laughing and crying now, holding his free hand, questioning and chattering but Will hardly registered.

'I'll take the horse to the stable Mother,' he said.

'Hurry back and tell us all your news. You must have had so many adventures ...'

Her voice faded as Will walked the horse round to the stables, unsaddled him and rubbed him down, then fed and watered him. By the time he got back to the house, both his parents were waiting for him in the warmth of the farmhouse kitchen where his mother was bustling around finding food and drink for him.

The scene was so comforting in its domesticity that he found it impossible to begin to tell them the news and stood awkwardly, his head bowed, watching his mother as she moved hither and thither fussing and chatting while his father looked on fondly.

At last Will cleared his throat. 'Father, mother ...'

They stopped then, picking up on the tone of his voice, and looked at him questioningly. His father frowned.

'What is it Will? Is something amiss?'

Chapter Two

Will swallowed but did not drop his gaze.

'I have been dismissed from my regiment in disgrace and Jack is dead.'

It was a brutal statement and he could hardly bear the expressions which passed over his parents' faces, first of disbelief then of horror and shock.

Still staring at him, his mother sat down suddenly at the table but his father remained standing, his face hard.

'Tell us how this came about,' he said quietly.

And so, Will began, haltingly at first, knowing how impossible they would find it to understand how his own fortunes had reversed so suddenly and how he had unwittingly played a part in his brother's death. He told them how he had been falsely accused of cowardice and insubordination and of his summary dismissal from the regiment. Then of his return to London to find that Jack had vanished and of how he, Will, had been set up as a decoy to lead Jack's enemies to his hiding place. How Jack had been shot and how Will had killed Jack's murderer. He did not tell them of Jack's true work, running a network of spies for King George's Government, nor that he, Will, had now been recruited by the Alien Office to continue that work. Nor did he tell them that Jack had been murdered because he had proof of the treachery of an important man in Government; nor that Jack's killer was a colleague who he had always trusted, who had been shamefully blackmailed by that traitor.

He told them the barest facts. And said to them that Jack had died in the service of his country.

When he had finished, no one spoke and the old farmhouse clock ticked into the silence.

At last, his mother whispered. 'What of Clara? Does Clara know?'

Will nodded. 'I have seen Clara and she knows what happened. She, too, has come home to break the news to her family.'

'So you travelled together?'

Will shook his head. 'No,' he said shortly. 'She cannot bear my presence. She cannot forgive me for my part in this sorry business.' He hesitated, then said quietly, 'indeed, I cannot forgive myself.'

'She and Jack were married only a matter of weeks and you are telling us that now the poor girl is a widow?'

Will said nothing.

His father cleared his throat. 'Had news of their marriage reached you? Jack said he had sent word.'

'No,' said Will. 'I only discovered on my return from Portugal.'

There was a dismal silence, his mother picking at the wool of her shawl and his father standing, head bent, staring down at the stone flags on the kitchen floor. After a few moments he looked up.

'I did hear a rumour,' he said at last.

Will's mother raised her head. 'A rumour? You said nothing to me of this.'

'What rumour, Father?' asked Will.

His father sighed. 'Spread by a landowner in Northumberland.'

Will closed his eyes. He knew exactly to whom his father referred. The man was the father of the officer who had accused Will of cowardice and insubordination.

'Do you know of whom I speak, Will?'

Will nodded. 'I served with his son. It was he who caused my disgrace.'

'Then the rumour was not unfounded. I have to admit that I dismissed it as idle gossip for I have no time for the man who spread it.'

Will straightened his back and looked his father in the eyes. 'I swear to you, Father, that these were false accusations.'

'Then how, in God's name, did it come to this, Will? How can your life have been ruined by a falsehood?'

'Because I left my post in the heat of battle,' he said quietly and, when his father began to speak, he held up his hand. 'Hear me out, please. I left a competent Lieutenant in charge and I only absented myself for long enough to go to the aid of my Sergeant who was sorely wounded. If I had not, he would have died.'

There was silence in the room, then Will continued. 'Sergeant Armstrong is a man who I would trust with my life and he has been at my side ever since I joined the Regiment.'

There was a long silence. Will's mother had turned her head away from the others and was weeping softly.

Then his father spoke again. 'And there was some talk of a duel?'

'I make no excuses there. Suffice to say that I was forced into it and it was witnessed by … by those who chose to report it.'

'Then it is true that the practice has been outlawed.'

Will gave a humourless laugh. 'It has, but Wellington himself has been known to challenge men to a duel.'

His father frowned. 'So, it still goes on?'

Will nodded. 'Occasionally, and those involved are given a reprimand, or a blind eye is turned. It is seldom reported.'

'But in your case?'

'Reported by the man who wished me ill.' Then, before his father could question him further, he continued. 'A vindictive and jealous bastard.'

'The son of the landowner of whom I spoke?'

'Yes,' muttered Will. He said nothing more. He was not going to burden his parents with the reason for the man's jealousy.

His father's shoulders slumped.

Will walked over to him and put a hand on his arm. 'I am so sorry, Father. After all you did for me. I know the sacrifice you made to find the money to buy my commission. I wish with all my heart that it had not come to this.'

His father raised his head and Will saw then how much he had aged. He had always been so strong and robust, a farmer through and through, out in all weathers, caring for the land and the beasts, but now it seemed that he had shrunk, both physically and spiritually.'

He is broken by this news. My disgrace and Jack's death. There is nothing I can say to comfort him. To comfort my mother.

The kitchen clock continued to tick loudly, relentlessly, and Will glanced at it, unreasonably angry at its indifference.

Time. If only time could be turned back. But it cannot and I must do my best to make my parents proud of me again.

He held his father away from him and looked into his eyes. 'I swear to you that I will do everything in my power to clear my name, Father.'

His father simply shook his head. 'The man's from a powerful family, Will.'

'And I was a good soldier, Father, and respected by the men I led. I will not have my name dragged through the mud by an incompetent fool, even though he is well bred and has powerful relations. He should never have been an officer. He was no leader of men.'

'Fighting talk my boy.' And there was a ghost of a smile.

Then, his mother looked up. 'Did Jack have a Christian burial?'

Will hesitated, remembering vividly the scene in that French wood. He knew that it would comfort her a little to know that Jack had been buried with some dignity.

'I buried him myself, Mother. And Sergeant Armstrong and I said a prayer over his grave.'

'At least you were with him. But how I wish that he was buried here in the village churchyard.'

Will said nothing. He would not tell them that Jack was buried alongside his murderer or that he and the Sergeant had prayed over that grave, too. The grave of a brilliant man, who had served his country well until he was blackmailed by a traitor.

The next few days were hard. Will had had more time to absorb his grief, but it was etched so clearly on the faces of his parents that he sometimes had to turn away from them. He helped his father around the farm with Winter repair jobs, taking some pleasure in physical labour while his mother continued with her household chores, though she would often be seen standing still, holding some kitchen implement and staring into the distance, alone with her thoughts. Over meals at the kitchen table, they spoke about Jack and Clara and Will was able to tell them a little about the apartment Jack had found in Lincoln's Inn and how Clara had already put her feminine touches upon it. He told them nothing of Jack's other lodging place where some of his dubious informants had been to visit him.

10

'I hope that Clara will find it in her heart to forgive you, Will,' said his mother. 'It is all so shocking for the poor girl.'

Will shook his head. 'I doubt she'll ever forgive me, but she can attach no blame to you and father. I'm sure that once I have left, she will visit you.'

This was the first time he had talked of leaving though he had assumed that they would not expect him to stay for long.

'So, you are determined on making your life in London?' asked his father.

Will crumbled a piece of bread between his fingers.

Is he disappointed? Had he hoped that I would stay here and help him?

'Yes,' he said. 'I shall travel back to London shortly. I have been promised employment there.'

They both looked up then. 'You have said nothing of this. What sort of employment?'

Will hesitated. 'I will be serving my country in a different way,' he said.

'But not as a soldier?'

'No. Though if I could ever clear my name and be accepted back into the Regiment, I would dearly love to return.'

'Then what ...?'

'I shall be working for the Government as ... in a different capacity.'

His father frowned. 'In the manner in which Jack worked for the Government?'

Will nodded.

He is shrewd. Jack would never have told him the nature of his work, but I don't doubt that he has guessed.

A few days after this conversation, Will left the farm. He was well-rested and had clean apparel and the day was crisp and clear but none of this served to lift his spirits as he headed down the track. Before he reached the gate, he turned in his saddle and looked back to see his parents still standing at the farmhouse door, his father's arm round the shoulders of his mother, watching him. He felt the tears prick at his eyes, then he raised his hand in farewell, urged the cob forward and trotted off up the track.

There had been no word from Clara while he had been staying at his parents' farm even though they had been separated by less than a mile, and he had not dared to contact her. He entertained a faint hope that she, too, might be on the stagecoach going South from Durham and that they could at least speak together, but it was not to be. As he stood outside the Three Tuns Inn the following morning, watching the coach slithering down the hill towards him, she was not among those waiting to board.

Chapter Three

It was not until the beginning of the New Year that Will was summoned to the Alien Office. He had returned to London from the North fully expecting to be set to work immediately but, although he had received some money, there had been no other word.

He went back to Mrs Baxter's lodging house in Drury Lane, though he was nervous that he would not be welcomed there after the scandal he had caused. But, surprisingly (and, no doubt, because she had an empty room she wished to fill and because he offered to pay monthly in advance) she greeted him, if not with enthusiasm, at least with a measure of civility. He was grateful to be back in familiar surroundings.

Will knew that Clara's family had invited his own parents to be with them to celebrate Christmas and though it would, no doubt, be a solemn gathering, he was glad for them – and glad that he had decided to return to London. They would not have been invited if he had continued to stay with them at the farm.

So Will spent Christmas at the house in Drury Lane, with the laundress and her husband and baby, who lodged in Mrs Baxter's downstairs back bedroom, with Betsy, the servant girl, and with Mrs Baxter and her sister. The sister was a widow and had come up from the country. She was more forthcoming and less sour than Mrs B, and at first Will found her company entertaining, but after a few days the constant empty chatter began to grate and he longed for the return of the two actresses, Sally and Lottie, who had gone to their respective families for the celebrations.

He could not help but remember past Christmases. Christmases with Jack and his parents and their neighbours at the farm with all the food and merriment, or, in other years, in the company of the men of his regiment.

These memories came back even more strongly when Sergeant Armstrong persuaded Will to join him from time to time over the festive period. Armstrong had returned to his lodging in Seven Dials where the ribald and ale fuelled celebrations at the Haycart tavern suited him well and where there were a few others like him – wounded soldiers returned from the war.

'You need company, sir,' Armstrong said to Will. 'Company stops you brooding and you'll be no good to man or beast if you keep thinking on what is past.'

'Stop calling me sir.'

'Aye, sir,' said Armstrong, grinning, glad to see a faint smile on Will's face.

They were sitting together in the crowded room at the Haycart which was thick with smoke and the odour of unwashed bodies and stale ale.

'You should move out of Seven Dials,' said Will. 'It's a den of thieves and you have money enough to afford somewhere better.'

'That's what Sal says.'

'And she's right.' Will took another sup of ale. 'I'm surprised she still puts up with your company. I can't imagine what she sees in you.'

Armstrong grinned. 'We get along well, me and Sal. We understand each other.'

'Then you should take notice of her. It's a dangerous place. It's naught but a rookery.'

Armstrong scratched the stump of his arm. 'Truth to tell, I like it here, sir. I've got used to it. The company's rough but it suits me.' Then he put his finger to the side of his nose and winked at Will. 'And remember, sir, you gleaned a deal of intelligence from here – about smugglers and the like.'

Will had to acknowledge the truth of this. He had picked up intelligence here which had led him to smugglers in Hastings who took not only contraband goods over the Channel to France, but also spies. And the smugglers didn't ask any questions. It was not their business to ask for whom the spies worked.

Yet if I had not found out about the goods and people moved to and fro, I may not have found Jack's hiding place and he might yet be alive.

But he didn't voice these thoughts. He watched as Armstrong struggled to get tobacco and a clay pipe out from his pocket, then Will stretched over, took the pipe from him, packed it with tobacco for him and lit it. Armstrong drew on it and puffed out a curl of smoke.

'When do we start work, sir?'

Will shrugged. 'When I get word, I'll tell you Sergeant.' He did not wish to make any mention of the Alien Office in these surroundings. Armstrong understood and nodded.

'A waiting game then, is it?'

'It would seem so.'

'I must admit to being impatient to start.'

'As am I,' said Will.

***

Then, at last the call came and Will and Armstrong found themselves waiting in the lobby of The Alien Office. Though officially a part of the Home Office, the Alien Office was not situated in Whitehall but in Crown Street in Westminster.

At length they were ushered into the office of John Reeves. It was a pleasant light room with heavy drapes at the windows. A large solid desk stood in front of the windows and a merry fire blazed in the grate. A welcome contrast to the cold lobby at the entrance to the building.

Reeves, the head of the Alien Office, stood up to greet them. He was a formidable figure; a legal man who had held several important Government roles both at home and abroad. He was given to long and somewhat unnerving silences as he pondered things, sniffing snuff up his nostrils as he did so. Will had met him previously, indeed had been recruited by him, a completely unexpected turn of events which had effectively saved him from penury and imprisonment. Although at first, Will had been somewhat overawed by the man, he liked and respected him and he knew how well he had thought of Jack.

Duncan Armstrong, however, was ill at ease. He shifted his feet and stared down at the fine turkey carpet on the floor, as Reeves silently scrutinised him. Reeves looked him up and down, saying nothing but frowning, his hands clasped behind his back.

Will prayed silently that Armstrong would pass whatever test he was being given. After all, he, Will, had insisted that Armstrong be recruited. What if Reeves found him wanting?

'I hear you fought bravely in the Peninsular, Sergeant.'

'I hope I did my duty, sir,' muttered Armstrong, still looking down at the carpet.

'And you were wounded in the process,' said Reeves, gesturing towards Armstrong's empty sleeve. 'No small sacrifice.'

Reeves turned to Will. 'And you say that the Sergeant was your right-hand man?'

'An unfortunate turn of phrase, sir,' said Will.

Reeves frowned. 'Ah, yes, I see what you mean.' A slight smile flickered over his face.

Will continued. 'He was an excellent soldier and when we returned from Portugal and were sent on the assignment by James Montagu, he was my eyes and ears, picking up information I could not. He is resourceful and utterly to be trusted.'

Reeves addressed Armstrong. 'If you are to join us, Sergeant, you may have to extricate yourself from difficult situations and take flight at a moment's notice. Do you not feel that you might be hampered by your …?' He pointed at Armstrong's missing arm.

'I can use a dagger in my left hand, sir,' said Armstrong. 'And my wits ain't been affected.'

Reeves' lips twitched. 'That I can believe.'

Then he started to pace up and down saying nothing while Will and Armstrong stood, somewhat awkwardly, watching him. At length, he came to a stop in front of them.

'As you can imagine, Sergeant,' he said. 'I have looked into your background thoroughly and I am minded to trust you but, as you know, lately my trust has been betrayed so you will forgive my hesitancy.'

Then, after another session of frowning and staring, he suddenly clapped his hands.

'Very well gentlemen, let us get to work.'

He gestured for them to take chairs and sit at the large mahogany desk, then he gathered up the papers on it, put them to one side and unrolled a large map, anchoring it at each corner with paperweights. It was a map of France.

Will stood up and leant over the desk to look more closely at the map. He could see at once that there were clusters of numbers written on it.

Reeves tapped the map with his finger. 'The numbers relate to our agents' locations in France,' he said.

Will scrutinised the map. There were many numbers dotted around the Northern coastal towns and villages and more in towns further South and West and in Paris. He straightened up. 'I had no idea that the network was so extensive, sir. Are all these agents currently operative?'

'No,' said Reeves, shortly. 'Many of them have been uncovered due to the treachery of Vicomte de Menou.'

Armstrong frowned. 'Vicomte de Menou. Who's he?'

'An aristocrat who fled to England during the French Revolution. At that time, many who came here changed their names to sound more like Englishmen. While he was here he went under the name of Samuel Barker.'

'Ah,' said Will. 'That is a name I recognise. The traitor who blackmailed James Montagu.'

'Indeed,' said Reeves. 'The man deceived everyone. He rose to be a respected and influential man in our Government and was recruited to oversee part of the spy network here.'

'And all the time he was acting as a double agent,' finished Will.

'Bastard!' said Armstrong.

Reeves sighed. 'A clever bastard. He played a long game, wheedling himself into the good offices of highly placed Government officials and visiting ambassadors.'

Reeves cleared his throat and continued. 'Now we have to attempt to limit the damage that Barker has wrought. And this is where we shall need your help.'

'When we met before, sir, you mentioned rebuilding the network in France,' said Will.

'Indeed. But we also need to rescue those of our agents who have been identified by Barker and have not yet been run to earth by Joseph Fouché.'

'The Minister of Police in France?'

'Indeed. And he has charge of the secret police in Paris.' Reeves suddenly scraped back his chair and stood looking out of the window at the cold grey sky outside.

'Truly, gentlemen, I am aware, more than most, that all is said to be fair in love and war, but Fouché is a monster. He is a rabid Jacobin and any uprising against Napoleon is repressed with the utmost violence and cruelty.' He shuddered and went on speaking so quietly that it seemed that he was not addressing them but speaking to himself. 'The stories I have heard of his brutality sicken me.'

'So, you want our agents out of his clutches,' said Armstrong.

'Those who were known to Barker, yes, and have not yet been discovered by Fouché's men.'

'So Barker did not know of them all?'

Reeves sighed. 'Last year I had begun to suspect that we had a traitor within the network so I took it upon myself to personally recruit some new members and their identity is known only to me and to one or two trusted colleagues. For the time being, these new recruits should be safe but we need many more and we need to protect those who have been outed.'

'Getting them to safety sounds like mighty dangerous work, sir,' said Armstrong.

'Indeed, Sergeant.'

'But nothing that the Captain and I can't handle, I warrant.'

Sir John Reeves smiled broadly. 'And that is my belief, also, Sergeant.'

'So, where do we begin, sir?' asked Will. 'No doubt we shall be furnished with names and locations and codes and such like?'

'All of that, Will. And your work will begin as soon as you are fully briefed.'

He moved over to a table set against the wall on which stood a decanter of fortified wine and poured generous measures into three glasses. He handed one each to Will and Armstrong and raised his own.

'May God be with you in your mission, gentlemen,' he said, and they all raised their glasses.

'So it is back to France again,' said Will, glancing at Armstrong and remembering his fear of the sea.

'No,' said Reeves, slowly. 'Not France. At least not immediately.'

'Not France? But I understood you to say …' began Will.

Reeves nodded. 'All in good time, Will. But your mission begins in Jersey.'

'*Jersey,*' said Armstrong.

'It is one of the Channel Islands, Sergeant.'

'I know that,' muttered Armstrong, not entirely truthfully.

'And you will give no hint of your mission or of its whereabouts to anyone except those working for me. Is this clear?'

'Understood sir,' said Will.

'Aye,' said Armstrong.

Chapter Four

For the next few days, Will and Armstrong were briefed by Reeves and his colleagues. They began to understand the extent of the operation, of how the Alien Office worked with the post office to open, read and reseal letters from France. They learnt how letters in code were deciphered in the deciphering branch and how letters were planted in foreign embassies. They learnt about secret codes, passwords and invisible writing as well as certain signals from boats on the water or lights on land and what they meant. Will and Armstrong were astonished at the complexity of the operations, how royalist agents were armed and financed. Of the papermills that forged French paper with French watermarks. And how some agents were housed in the Home Office. They learnt about safe houses and landing places for spies and of some of the complicated arrangements made to support uprisings against the regime within France.

In any free time they had they shut themselves away in Will's room at his lodging house and went over everything they had been taught, again and again, conversing in low voices.

'I should feel more secure in this if we had some notes,' said Will. 'Something to refer to should we forget.'

'Nah!' said Armstrong. 'Between us we'll remember it all.'

'But to commit everything to memory. What if our memories fail?'

Armstrong repeated Reeves' mantra which had been drilled into them. '*Commit nothing to paper which is not in code. A spy's memory for facts and faces is his most important asset.*'

'Huh. My head is so full of facts that it is ready to burst. How can we absorb all this in just a few days? Has Reeves revealed to you when we are to begin?'

Will shook his head. 'I know no more than you do. When he feels we are ready no doubt.'

There was some distraction for the two men when Sally and Lottie returned to Mrs Baxter's house and regaled them with stories of their families' activities over the festive season. Will observed with amusement the expression on Duncan Armstrong's face as he and Sally were reunited and began to fling fond insults at each other. There was no doubt that Armstrong had fallen hard for the young actress and his affection did seem to be reciprocated.

Then the day came when Reeves considered that Will and Armstrong were ready to be sent off on their mission and Armstrong had the difficult task of telling Sally that he would be gone for some time. Will was about to absent himself from the room and give them some privacy, but Sally turned to him.

'You're going with him ain't you, sir?'

'Yes. We have … we are now working for the Government, Sal. We have to go where we are told.'

She looked from one to the other. 'This is all mixed up with Mr Jack's death, ain't it?'

Armstrong glanced at Will, who answered for him. 'I have taken on my brother's role, Sal,' he said quietly. 'And the Sergeant will be helping me.'

There was a heavy silence and then she said. 'Don't think me and Lottie don't know what you're doing. We helped disguise you, remember?'

'And an excellent job you did,' said Will.

'I know when to keep my lip buttoned,' she said. And then, with a flash of her old humour, she addressed Armstrong. 'What you're doing can't be much more dangerous than living in that hell hole in Seven Dials.'

Armstrong grinned. 'I'll miss you Sal,' he said.

'Well, I doubt we'll miss you, Duncan Armstrong. We'll be that busy at the theatre we'll not have time to think of you.'

Will had to turn away to hide his smile.

They had a last meeting with Reeves on the evening before they were to leave for Jersey. Until then, they'd been told nothing about who they were to contact. It was a vilely cold January evening. The sleet swirled around them as they made their way to the Alien Office and they paced up and down and stamped their feet to keep warm down in the cold lobby while they waited to be summoned. When they were admitted to his office at last they found Reeves in a gloomy mood.

'I have just now had bad news from Spain,' he said.

Will looked up. 'A defeat of our forces, sir?'

Reeves nodded. 'A defeat at La Coruña. And, worse still, Sir John Moore was killed on the battlefield.'

'The Commander of the British Army?' said Armstrong.

'The very same. A sorry blow. He was a fine man.'

They were all silent for a while, absorbing this information, then Reeves sighed. 'However, we have work to do,' he continued, and he then explained to them why they were to go to Jersey.

'We had an excellent agent in Jersey,' said Reeves. 'He went by the name of Gabriel and he made nearly two hundred trips to take messages to our agents in Normandy and bring back their information. He was one of our best and most loyal informants.'

'You speak of him in the past tense?' said Will.

'Yes. Sadly.'

'Was he caught?'

Reeves nodded. 'Caught by Fouché and executed.'

Will looked at the candles in the sconces round the wall, each sending out its own small pool of light.

Will that be our fate?

Reeves sighed. 'He was an exceptionally brave man – a fisherman by trade – and I have it on good authority that he did not break under torture.'

Armstrong glanced at Will. Both men wondering whether they would be brave enough to withstand the kind of cruelty meted out by the Minister of Police and his men.

'Gabriel revealed nothing to Fouché. He had a small group of associates in Jersey, mostly fishermen, and as yet, their names are not known to the French but there may well be French spies on the island who want to uncover them. You have been given the necessary codes and signals which will lead you to our agents. Seek out these loyal royalists with all haste and gain their trust. Once they are confident that you are working for us, they can furnish you with the kind of detailed information you need to start on your mission.'

'And we are to do this under the very noses of French spies?' asked Armstrong.

John Reeves shrugged. 'Possibly, but the islanders themselves are loyal to the British Crown.'

'And the garrison there is manned I believe?' said Will.

Reeves nodded. 'Yes, the island is in a vulnerable position, being so close to the French coast. It is well fortified and the 2nd Battalion of the 62nd Duke of Edinburgh's Wiltshires are there at the moment.'

Will turned to Armstrong. 'Some military company for you Sergeant.'

'Indeed,' said Reeve. 'Your presence there should arouse no suspicion. Many retired or wounded army and navy officers have immigrated to the island. They enjoy the cheap living there and the pleasant climate.' He paused to take a pinch of snuff. Then there was another of his long silences. Armstrong cleared his throat and shuffled his feet, Will stood up a little straighter.

'One more thing,' said Reeves at last.

The other two looked at him questioningly.

'While I sincerely hope that you will be able to ease the passage of our agents who need to flee France, there is another even more urgent task. One which will need all your ingenuity and acting skills.'

Will frowned. 'I have no acting skills, sir.'

'Not what I have heard. And I'm told you used them to good effect when your smuggler's vessel was apprehended by a gunboat.'

How can he know of that incident? The man is hellishly well informed.

Armstrong grinned. 'He missed his calling, sir. He should have been on the stage.'

Will shot him a warning glance and spoke to Reeves. 'Are we to be told of this more urgent task, sir?'

Reeves strode over to the window, parted the heavy drapes and stared out into the darkness, then let them drop and walked slowly back to the others.

'When de Menou …'

'The traitor Samuel Barker?'

'Aye. When he was uncovered, I did not think that he knew the real identity of who it was, in France, who was masterminding our network there. This person is known to the other agents as Gaston but their real name was a secret I'd kept very closely guarded and only shared with one or two most trusted colleagues.'

Will sensed what was coming. 'And was one of those trusted colleagues James Montagu, sir?'

'Unfortunately, yes.'

'And you think he may have revealed Gaston's identity to Barker?'

Reeves shrugged. 'I cannot know that but Barker would have been desperate to discover it.'

'And you have not heard from this Gaston?'

Reeves shook his head. 'Unusually, there has been no word since Montagu's death and de Menou's disappearance. Gaston appears to have vanished without trace and I suspect may be being held prisoner somewhere.'

'And this man Gaston would have more knowledge than any other of our network?' said Armstrong. 'Indeed, I can understand why you are so anxious to know what has happened to him.'

Reeves looked up. 'Her,' he said slowly. 'Not a man, Will. Gaston is a woman.'

'A woman!' repeated Will. 'Surely that is a mighty dangerous job for a woman?'

'She is an unusual woman. Clever, brave and resourceful and, until recently, completely unsuspected by Joseph Fouché and his henchmen. But I cannot know now if this is still the case.'

'And you want us to find out?' said Armstrong.

Reeves nodded. 'I have revealed to you that Gaston is a woman but you must swear to tell no-one.' He stared at them both. 'If it is still unknown to Fouché and she can continue her work for us, then do nothing. If it is not and she is in danger or has been captured, then I am charging you with her rescue.'

Will and Armstrong exchanged glances as they absorbed this information. They listened attentively as Reeves told them more about Gaston, how much she had done for them, the information she had gleaned from under the noses of influential people and of her boldness in doing so. And of her skill at handling the royalist spies from within France.

They had hardly had time to take this in when Reeves began to speak of more mundane and practical issues.

'You have thought through your cover story, no doubt, once you reach Jersey?'

'Visiting the island for recreation, sir.'

'Hmm. Make sure your story is sound, Will. Think it through carefully.'

There was a lull in the conversation, while both Will and Armstrong pondered the task ahead.

'Will they all speak English, sir?' asked Armstrong.

'Most of the islanders speak a form of French – a sort of patois.'

Armstrong frowned. 'My understanding of the language is not good, sir, but the Captain's fluent.'

'Speaking English on the island will not be remarked upon, Sergeant, but it will be a different matter when you step on French soil.' Reeves turned to Will. 'Perhaps the Sergeant could pretend severe deafness - or idiocy? – you will have to be imaginative.'

'We will give it some thought, sir,' said Will quickly, seeing Armstrong's expression. Then he added, 'Is there one person in particular we should seek out first when we reach the island?'

'I would recommend that you contact Gabriel's widow, Florence. By all accounts, she was fully apprised of his activities but pleads ignorance, for obvious reasons. Do not approach her openly. I'm sure you understand why. Leave a coded note at this drop-off point.' Reeves went over to his desk and spread a map of Jersey on its surface. 'Here,' he said, pointing at a mark on the map. 'There are sundry drop off points on the island and they move constantly. Use this one.' He pointed at the map. 'Memorise its position. There is a derelict cottage just above the main village of St Aubin. It still has its chimney intact. Hide your note in the chimney and wait for a reply. If necessary, she will tell you of other places where you can safely leave notes but ideally it is better not to do so after the initial contact.'

Will and Armstrong pored over the map for a while, memorising the exact location and noting certain landmarks.

Then Reeves advised them of the best way to travel to Jersey, wished them Godspeed and dismissed them but just as they were leaving, he looked up from the paper he was reading.

'You have not asked me how any agents you rescue will get over the channel?'

Will felt his cheeks redden. 'An oversight, sir.'

'There will be a galley in readiness,' he said. 'It will be in

English waters but in sight of the French coast at Le Trépot. The Master of the vessel will stay in those waters every day unless the seas are impossibly rough, beginning in three weeks from today. Our contact at Le Trépot will signal to him when he is needed and then he will come in to harbour.'

'And you are sure that this signaller is true? Has not been exposed?'

Reeves scratched his chin. 'I have no reason to doubt him,' he said. And then he gave them the man's name and how he could be contacted.

As they left the building, Armstrong turned to Will.

'A woman spy!' he said, his voice incredulous.

'I confess I was amazed,' said Will. 'But then perhaps a woman would not fall under suspicion in the same way as a man.'

'Maybe,' said Armstrong, rubbing his chin. 'But still, she must be a brave lady.' He pulled his cloak closer as they walked off, the sleet stinging their faces.

'So, it's off to the coast again, sir,' he muttered, after a while.

'I fear it is, Sergeant. But there's no other way to get to the Channel Islands.'

'My God, I hate the sea.'

Will didn't reply. His thoughts were fully occupied.

When I was fighting for my country my life was often in danger but then I was surrounded by comrades. The task ahead will be equally dangerous and Armstrong and I will have little support and will have to live on our wits. It is possible that we may not return. I have seen my parents and bid them farewell. I cannot leave without trying to make my peace with Clara – if she will let me.

He turned to Armstrong. 'I am going to visit Clara,' he said.

'Your brother's widow? Ain't it a bit late to go calling?'

Will sighed. They had an early start and he hesitated for a moment, thinking of his comfortable bed.

'Nonetheless,' said Will. 'I will try to see her before we leave. If the worst should happen.' Armstrong nodded into the darkness.

Chapter Five

It took a long time to find a hackney cab and the disgruntled driver, who was on his way home, needed some inducements to agree to take them. They were to leave from Will's lodgings in the morning so Armstrong was staying with him for the night and the driver dropped him off before conveying Will to Lincoln's Inn. Giving the man more coin to wait for him, Will looked up from the courtyard and saw that there was a light burning in

Clara's apartment and ran up the stone stairs to the second floor and, before his courage deserted him, knocked on the door.

He could hear movement inside and he guessed that Clara was alone, having sent her maid to bed. He knocked again, louder this time and at last a voice came from within.

'Who is it?' She sounded nervous.

'Clara, it is Will.'

There was silence.

'Please Clara. My pardon for calling so late but I am leaving London in the morning and I … I may not return.'

The silence continued.

'I crave just a few moments of your time, Clara. To bid you farewell.'

'I don't know Will …'

'Five minutes, Clara. I have a hackney below waiting.'

More silence and then he heard the bolt being slid back. She opened the door a fraction and stared out onto the unlit landing.

'May I come in?'

For answer she opened the door further. Will walked in and they stood looking at each other in the candlelit room. Even in the dim light he could sense the grief etched in her face and a whole maelstrom of emotions assailed him. His youthful passion for her, never truly extinguished despite her marriage to Jack, his guilt at his part in his brother's death and his own deep sorrow. He cleared his throat.

'I come to say goodbye, Clara.' He hesitated. 'My only wish is that we should part as friends.'

She moved over to sit in a chair by the fire whose flames were still flickering weakly, and gestured for him to sit opposite her.

She sighed. 'I have had much time to reflect, Will, and I have realised that in some ways I, too, was guilty of leading Montagu to Jack.'

Will frowned. 'No, you ...'

She held up her hand to silence him. 'If I had not discovered that note and had not ridden down to the coast to apprise you of its contents ...'

'Your bravery astonished me.'

'But if I had not ...'

Will leant forward and took her hand. 'We cannot look back on what we cannot change, Clara,' he said softly.

She shook her head and looked down at her lap.

'It was good to see your parents at Christmas, even though it was a sorrowful time. I am very fond of them, Will.'

'And they of you.'

'But what does life hold for me now? I could not bear to stay up North, yet here, without Jack, my life is restricted. I do not care for the social round but I do have friends who are kind to me and I suppose, when the better weather comes, I shall be able to ride in the park again, but it is such an empty life.' She withdrew her hand from his and looked up.

'You say you are to leave town in the morning.'

Will picked up the question in her voice. 'I have been asked to take Jack's place,' he said.

There was a long silence, then Clara sighed. 'So you, too, will become a spy,' she said.

He could not deny it so he said nothing.

'I suppose I cannot ask where you are going?'

Will smiled. 'You know I cannot say.'

'It will be fraught with danger, no doubt.'

'That is why I wanted to see you. In case ...'

'In case we do not meet again.'

He nodded and they were both silent for a while. Then Clara rose to her feet.

'Thank you for coming, Will. You were right to do so and I am glad we are not parting as enemies. She went to the window, spotting the lanterns on the hackney cab below. 'Your cab is still waiting.'

Will rose. 'My heart feels a deal lighter, Clara. Whatever lies ahead I hope that I shall face it with courage.' He reached the door and turned to her. 'Will you give me your blessing?'

'It is yours, Will.' Then she gave him a wry smile. 'Think of me in my dull life here while you are dodging death and catching spies.'

In the cab on the way back to Drury Lane, Will thought back to the dangerous journey Clara had taken, riding, disguised as a young man, all the way down to the coast to give him the coded message Jack had left for her.

Chapter Six

They left shortly after dawn the next morning to catch the stagecoach to Southampton. Will had persuaded his driver from the night before to take them. The streets were clear so that they drove Eastwards at a good pace and were soon at La Belle Sauvage, a large coaching inn at Ludgate Hill, with stabling for more than one hundred horses. Even at this early hour there was a crowd of people shouting and shoving and loading luggage. The night guard dogs were being rounded up and caged and coaches were already leaving the inn.

It was a long journey to Southampton but the weather had cleared and, once over the Thames, the fog of choking smoke was behind them. They stopped several times at inns to change horses, to relieve themselves, to take a little refreshment and to stretch their aching limbs. But they never tarried long and reached the coast well before midnight where they put up at the appropriately named Coach and Horses Inn.

Conscious of their mission, they had not got into conversation with fellow passengers on the coach. Neither did they fraternise with other guests at the Coach and Horses, but kept their own counsel. If they were asked about their journey they made vague replies about visiting relations in Southampton.

First thing the next morning, Armstrong set out to enquire about getting passage over to Jersey and he'd been gone less than half an hour before he returned to the inn with all haste.

'There's a packet leaving within the hour, sir, taking mail to the island,' he said, breathing heavily. 'She's called *The Rose*. Master's name is de Gruchy, which sounds mighty Frenchified to me, but he spoke decent English. Told me that the vessel's armed with four guns and that he carries passengers. *And* that the charge to take us over is one pound and one shilling each!'

Will raised an eyebrow. 'That's mighty steep, Sergeant, but it sounds a safe way to travel. You reserved us a berth I hope?'

Armstrong nodded. 'Aye, though it pained me to part with so much coin.'

'Good,' said Will. 'Then we shall soon begin our work.'

'If we miss this packet, there's not another for a few days, de Gruchy said. They don't go that regular.'

It took them little time to pack their scant belongings and settle their bill. Along with a few garments and some other provisions, they had between them two pistols, a short sword and a dagger concealed at the bottom of Will's haversack. He slung the haversack over his shoulder and followed Armstrong down the cobbled streets to the harbour.

As they climbed aboard *The Rose* the greeting from the Master was perfunctory. One of the crew showed them to a berth but there was no time for social intercourse. All was hustle and bustle as the vessel was readied for sail. Cargo and mail for the island were being loaded on board, sailors were shouting instructions, one to another, and before long, sails were hoisted and they were on their way out of Southampton Water and making for the Channel. Once they were on their way, Will and Armstrong went up on deck and it was not long before Armstrong had voided his stomach over the rails.

It was a bleak, cold morning and as Will looked about him he thought back to when they had been in these waters only a few months ago when he and the Sergeant had returned to England from Portugal on the hospital ship.

What changes we have experienced in those few short months.

Armstrong's face was ashen. 'I had thought I might have been cured by now,' he muttered. 'Still, it's not a long journey, across the Channel.'

Will did not have the heart to tell him that the voyage would be much longer than the one they had undertaken previously, from Hastings to Gravelines.

'It's a more stable vessel, too, Sergeant. And it's legal,' he added, smiling.

They were both thinking of the smuggler who had taken them to Gravelines when an English gunboat had accosted them.

Once they were in the open water of the Channel, a North-Easterly wind got up and although it filled the sails it penetrated through their garments and chilled them to the bone so that they soon went below. Armstrong said little and it was obvious he was feeling wretched. Will tried to rest, to conserve his energy, but there was too much swirling around his head to relax and in truth, though he was not prone to seasickness, the voyage was far from comfortable in the Winter seas.

The short January day began to fade and by five in the evening it was inky dark. *The Rose* sailed on, lanterns on her prow dipping as she climbed up one wave only to slide down into the valley between that and the next.

Will must have slept eventually, through sheer exhaustion, and when he awoke, he went up on deck. It took him a moment to realise that *The Rose* was no longer making any headway but simply rocking to and fro and that her sails had been lowered. He frowned, not understanding the reason. Spotting one of the sailors who was coiling some ropes, he asked why they had anchored.

'Waiting for dawn, sir,' said the man. 'Landing at St Helier's too shallow on this tide. Once it's light you'll be taken ashore on the tender.'

Will stood looking out towards the island whose shape he could just discern as the sky lightened. Although he was wearing a heavy wool coat, he still shivered and rubbed his hands together to try and warm himself. He knew there were fortifications on the island, some manned towers at strategic points and the famous Elizabeth Castle in St Aubin's bay where the military were currently garrisoned. Gradually he began to see more detail and it seemed to him that, with its steep rocky sides contrasting with sandy beaches, that there would be plenty of places of concealment.

At length he was joined by Armstrong. The Sergeant was still looking miserable but he cheered up when Will told him it would not be long before they were conveyed to the shore by tender.

'Lord, I'll be glad to have solid land beneath my feet again.'

They stood together watching the movements of the crew, as dawn broke, lowering the wooden tender into the water, filling it with packages and goods for the island first, and then urging Will and Armstrong and the other two passengers to get into it. Armstrong went first, hanging grimly onto the rope ladder with his one arm and landing, rockily, into the boat, then Will followed, his rucksack on his back, and sat beside the Sergeant as two sailors rowed the boat to the landing stage.

Once they were on the sandy beach, Armstrong turned to Will. 'We will need to find some transport, will we not, to St Aubin.'

Will had been minded to walk across the sands at low tide to the fishing village of St Aubin, which he knew from memorising the map was not far distant, but looking at Armstrong's grey face, he took pity on the man and agreed.

As it was Saturday, market day, there were stallholders preparing to sell their wares and the early buyers were already gathering around. When they enquired about transport to St Aubin they were told that a horse drawn omnibus went to and fro on market day, from the Bunch of Grapes tavern in Water Lane to the Swift Tavern in St Aubin. They made their way to The Bunch of Grapes and it wasn't long before they saw the omnibus approach. After its passengers had alighted and the driver taken a short rest, Will and Armstrong climbed aboard, perched beside one another on one of the outside seats on top of the vehicle. After a while, the team of four horses set off back for St Aubin.

The fare was ten sous and they had been well provided with French francs by Reeves' men.

'We'll have to get used to dealing in francs and sous now Sergeant,' whispered Will after he had handed over the money.

'And the language,' muttered Armstrong. 'You seem to understand them sir, but I'm buggered if I can.'

'I can only just make it out myself. It's a mixture of French and their own patois. They have many of their own words for things and these words are not familiar to me.'

As they left the town of St Helier, Will remarked to one of the other passengers on the narrowness of the road and that it seemed sunken down below the land and overhung with trees.

'Getting about the island must be difficult,' he said.

The other passenger shrugged. 'That's all changing,' the man said. 'The military are building better roads on the orders of the island's Governor.' He gave a short laugh. 'At first there was a deal of trouble from the landowners but I reckon they've come round now and can see their value.' He paused. 'The soldiers are

33

already at work constructing more, to link the harbour with the military fortifications – and a new fort, I'm told.'

'A good use of their time no doubt,' said Will.

'Yes, indeed. Nothing much going on for them here. Leastways, there's no fighting.'

'But I'll warrant the islanders are glad of their presence, nonetheless.'

Even from their perch on top of the omnibus, Will and Armstrong could see little of the layout of the island and it was difficult to get any sense of direction as the narrow, sunken road twisted and turned.

Their companion continued to chatter on, warning them that strangers could easily get lost and confused and urging them to employ a guide if they were to explore the island.

'You say you are here for a holiday?'

'And to see whether perhaps I might settle here,' said Will quickly. 'Sergeant Armstrong and I have left the army and I'm told the climate is mild and the living cheap. We are looking for a quiet life.'

Armstrong had to turn away to hide his smile as the man continued to question them.

'I can see why the Sergeant can no longer fight,' he said. 'But you are young and fit sir, surely …'

'My wounds are not visible,' said Will, shortly, and after that their companion fell into an embarrassed silence.

The journey to St Aubin was not far, just the other side of the bay from St Helier and before long the road dropped back down to the great sweep of St Aubin bay. They could see the fort of Elizabeth Castle looming up on an island on the other side of the bay and evidence of the fishing industry was all around – fishermen's cottages, boats, nets, peope going to and fro with boxes of their catch, loading them onto carts – the place was a hive of activity. As they drew closer, Armstrong nudged Will.

'Turn your eyes to the right, sir,' he whispered, 'look, beyond the cottages, a little higher up the hill.'

Will looked to where Armstrong indicated and saw a small cluster of ruined buildings. Most only had the remains of walls but there was one where a chimney stack still remained.

'Well spotted, Sergeant.'

'Do you reckon that's the one?'

Will nodded. 'Can't see any other,' he whispered, 'and it's in the right location is it not?'

At length, the omnibus drew up outside the Swift Tavern on the seafront and the passengers disembarked. There was already a cluster of folk waiting to make the return journey, most loaded down with goods to sell, all eager to get to the market at St Helier and there were many more, now that the tide had receded, walking to the market across the bay. And Armstrong pointed out, in the distance, a company of soldiers being drilled on the sands, too.

Will shaded his eyes and peered at the familiar red uniforms.

'Wish you were with them sir?'

Will did not answer him but busied himself disembarking from the omnibus.

They managed to find some accommodation at the Swift tavern, though it was very rudimentary and as soon as they had made the arrangements and had some refreshment, they repaired to their room and Will composed a short note written in the code taught to him by Reeves' men before they set off to do a little reconnaissance.

To the casual observer, they were two unremarkable young men, dressed in warm cloaks and stout boots, taking the air and exploring the island. They walked up behind the bay and passed the group of ruined buildings but did not stop there. Although there were not many people about, they judged it prudent to wait until they could be sure of being unobserved to leave the note. Reeves had impressed on them the need for caution and that any carelessness could put others in jeopardy.

They spent the rest of the day getting a feel for the place, mentally noting where boats might land unseen from prying eyes, watching the movement of the fishermen and women in the bay and whenever they met people who questioned them, reinforcing the story they had concocted to justify their presence on the island.

Chapter Seven

They had been well briefed by Reeves and knew the dimensions of the island and its main landmarks. They set themselves the task of walking the five miles from South to North. On several occasions they came across groups of the military moving carts containing materials for road building and, at one point, Armstrong got into conversation with a fellow sergeant supervising the men while Will walked on ahead not wanting to become involved. When Armstrong caught him up, he was full of enthusiasm.

'They'll have finished the first new road soon,' he said. 'The sergeant there told me it goes from St Helier to a place on the East called Grouville. And then they'll build more. And a new fort is planned.'

'It seems the soldiers are well occupied,' said Will. He smiled. 'I sense you enjoyed your exchange, Sergeant.'

'Always good to talk to fellow soldiers.' He paused and looked back at the group. 'The fellow said I'd be welcome to visit the fort at Castle Elizabeth,' he said.

Will shook his head. 'Better not, Sergeant. Remember why we're here.'

Armstrong looked momentarily crestfallen but then nodded. 'No doubt there'll be other excitements,' he said.

'I doubt we'll lack for excitement in the weeks to come.'

The light was already fading when they returned from their reconnaissance and they were tired and hungry. As they approached the derelict cottages, they could see no one in the vicinity and, indeed, most folk, it seemed, had already retired as there were lights twinkling in the homes of the fishermen and other inhabitants of St Aubin. Casually, Armstrong sat on the low wall of one of the collapsed buildings and, with some difficulty, managed to light his pipe while Will disappeared into the cottage with the still standing chimney. Once inside, he understood why it had been chosen as a hiding place. The walls were still tall enough to conceal you from sight once you had entered and only the birds above would be able to witness someone going over to the old fireplace. Quickly, Will felt for the first ledge inside the chimney and placed his coded note on it, as he'd been instructed, then slipped outside again to join Armstrong and they sauntered into the main village.

Armstrong looked back, frowning. 'Will it be picked up? Will anyone know it's there?'

'All we can do is to trust Reeves' instructions,' said Will. 'And wait.'

Although the accommodation at the Swift Tavern was rough it suited them well enough and they both slept heavily having dined, unsurprisingly, on a fish supper.

The next morning they conversed briefly with the landlord asking his advice about where they might settle should they come to live on the island, reinforcing their false identities. They thanked him for his courtesy and made sure they examined the village of St Aubin first, a place which he had, naturally, thoroughly recommended to them.

The tide was in so there were no soldiers drilling and no-one walking back to St Helier. There were a few fishing boats drawn up above the tide line but most were already out to sea and Will shaded his eyes and observed them, wondering which might be the fishermen who took letters and spies across the water to France.

'What should we do now?' asked Armstrong. 'Is it too early to go back to the hiding place?'

Will looked up towards the derelict cottages. 'I think we should wait a while. There are people about who would notice us.' He stretched and yawned. 'I have a fancy to see the Castle of Mont Orgueil, over to the East,' he said.

Armstrong knew why. They had both been told of its history by Reeves. It had once been the headquarters of the spy network here to where aristocrats fled at the time of the Revolution.

Will clapped Armstrong on the shoulder. 'Do you feel like a walk? By all accounts the castle has a mighty fine view across to France,' he said, smiling. 'Apparently it has cliffs on three sides and the sea on the fourth. A veritable fortress.'

'No good against an onslaught of cannon, though,' said

Armstrong. 'And,' he added, 'You know as well as I, sir, that it is too far to walk there and back in a day. Unless you're planning a route march.'

'Aye, you are right, Sergeant. It's just that I am restless. Until we have made contact with this fisherman's widow, we cannot usefully move forward.'

Instead, they walked back along the sunken road to St Helier. They paced up and down its narrow streets and took a jug of ale at The Bunch of Grapes and made some desultory enquiries about houses to rent. And when they noted that the tide had gone out, they walked back over the hard, damp sand.

Once it seemed that the population of St Aubin were safely inside their homes again, they made their way back to the derelict buildings before the winter light completely faded and, as before, Armstrong sat at lookout on the low wall when Will crept inside. He felt up to the shelf inside the chimney, once more, and felt the scrap of paper. Assuming that it was the one he had left there, he was about to turn away, but then he took it out. It was not the one he had written. It was too dark to see what was written on it so he put it in the pocket of his cloak and hurried out to Armstrong.

'We have an answer,' he whispered, and sat down beside him. The light was so bad that they had difficulty in seeing the writing but at length worked out the meaning.

Will stood up at once. 'Come on Sergeant. No time to waste. It seems we have already missed our appointed hour.'

Armstrong scrambled to his feet, grinning into the darkness.

***

Gabriel's widow, Florence, lived in a cottage at the end of a row, facing out to sea. As instructed, they approached it from behind, feeling their way in the darkness and moving as silently as they were able, and when they reached it Will knocked softly on the door four times, paused, then knocked again three times. She had obviously been expecting them for no sooner had the knocking finished than the door opened a crack and a faint light spilled out onto the lane. They could only see an outline of the woman who ushered them in with all haste and closed the door behind them.

It was a small cottage, sparsely furnished. The woman did not speak but took them immediately into the room at the front where a fire burned in the grate. As their eyes adjusted to the soft light of candles, they saw that there were four men in the room, all standing and peering at them in silence.

Will cleared his throat. 'Thank you for seeing us, Madame. My name is …'

Florence put up her hand. 'We go by false names, sir. It is better we do not know your true identity.'

One of the men stepped forward. 'A bad day for fishing,' he said, his voice low.

His accent was so thick that it took Will a moment to interpret the remark and remember the reply.

'And the boat leaks,' he said.

They seemed to have passed the test for at once Florence gestured at them to sit down, though there was precious little room and Will and Armstrong squeezed themselves in beside two men on a low settle.

'We are very sorry to hear of your husband's death,' said Will, addressing Florence who was still standing. 'By all accounts he was a truly brave man.'

She acknowledged his remark with a nod and there was a murmur among the men. 'The bravest,' said one of them.

Will took a moment to observe Florence. Even in the dim light he could see that a lifetime of hard work was evidenced in her gnarled hands and lined face but she stood upright and had a quiet dignity.

Does she know what her husband endured at the hands of Fouché's men? How can she bear it? She is much to be admired in continuing to support his work.

Then one of the others spoke. 'I returned from the Normandy coast only yesterday,' he said. 'I can give you recent intelligence.'

He then went on to the most recent news of which safe houses were no longer used, which drop off points had been changed and which contacts had disappeared for fear of discovery. Most of this intelligence had already reached the Alien Office, but there were some very recent developments and Will listened intently, making himself commit all the information to memory. He pondered whether he should mention their main mission and, after some hesitation, approached the subject in a roundabout way.

'Is there any news of Gaston?' he asked.

Immediately, all eyes were on him and he wondered if he had crossed a line. He glanced at Armstrong who shrugged.

There was some whispering among the men and some urgent gesticulating. Then the man recently returned from Normandy spoke again. 'It is rumoured that he is captured and is held somewhere outside Paris,' said the man. 'Though it is naught but rumour.'

It seems that even these true royalists do not know that Gaston is a woman then?

'And the rumour was not more specific?'

The man shook his head. 'Though it came from Pipette and she is normally to be relied upon.'

'Pipette?'

There was some more murmuring among the men who seemed to think that Will and Armstrong should know of Pipette and, before saying more, they began to question them more closely. Will disclosed as much as he felt he could and quoted John Reeves' instructions. There was more muttering and an uneasy few minutes while Will and Armstrong stood slightly apart.

'If we are not trusted by them, sir,' whispered Armstrong, 'our mission is doomed from the start.'

Will did not answer but continued to watch the men closely and, all the while, Florence stood, her arms folded and her body erect, staring at the group, and, in the end it was she who broke the silence.

'Enough! We waste time and gatherings here in my cottage are dangerous.' Then she turned to Will and Armstrong. 'Since my husband's death, you must understand that we have had to be a deal more careful about who to trust. It is only that they are surprised that you were not made aware of Pipette's activities.' Then she frowned. 'Though it may be that even those in London are unaware of them.'

'Aye,' said one of the men, overhearing her. 'That may be true. Her identity is known to us and to the fishing community over the water but it may not have reached those high up people in London.'

The atmosphere all of a sudden became less tense then and the men, after a few more whisperings among themselves, urged their spokesmen to address Will and Armstrong.

'Forgive us for doubting you, gentlemen,' he said. Then he cleared his throat and continued.

'Pipette is the wife of a French fisherman and she and her husband are both committed royalists and have run many risks for those determined to overthrow Napoleon. Pipette takes fish to the town market most days where she runs a stall and in this way she can communicate with many people outside her own village, without a shred of suspicion falling upon her. Along this coast, she is the link between spies bringing letters and gold – and even, on occasion, weapons – to pass on to the groups of royalist activists. She presents as being a dullard of a fishwife but in reality she's as sharp as a dagger and has a fine memory for faces and passwords.'

'Aye,' said another of the men. 'And her husband and his friends are all in it, too. We often bury goods in the sand on the uninhabited islets just off the French coast and folk will pick them up and hand them on to Pipette who passes them on to royalist contacts in amongst the crush and busy-ness of the market. If a fellow or some good woman goes off with more than a parcel of fish, who is to notice!'

There was a ripple of laughter among the assembled company, then Will broke in.

'That must need a deal of organisation,' he remarked. 'And involve much danger,' he added quietly.

Florence nodded. 'We cannot know how my Gabriel was apprehended. We only know that he gave away none of our secrets to Fouché's thugs, otherwise you can be sure they would have rounded us all up by now.'

'But I am guessing it has made them more suspicious of you?'

'Naturally,' said Florence. 'Which is why, sir, you and your friend here must take every care not to lead them to us.'

'Madame,' said Will. 'I swear that we shall be as vigilant as possible. We shall not betray your trust in us.'

'Good,' she said. 'See that you do not. There are many lives at stake.'

It was obvious that Florence was becoming increasingly anxious so an arrangement was quickly made for Will and Armstrong to travel over to the French coast the next night.

Chapter Eight

Will and Armstrong were the last to leave the cottage. Florence had insisted that the men left singly, thus drawing less attention to themselves. As she opened the back door for them, she put her hand on Will's arm. 'Bonne chance,' she whispered.

Will grabbed her hand and put it to his lips.

'You are an exceptional woman, Florence,' he muttered. 'I salute you for your fortitude.'

She did not reply but released her hand and closed the door softly and, of a sudden, they were alone in the dark.

They did not speak as they felt their way up the path behind the cottage and then along the bay back to the Swift Tavern. Just before they reached the entrance to the tavern, Armstrong turned to Will. 'What story do we tell, sir, should we be questioned?' he whispered.

Will stroked his chin. 'Thank you, Sergeant. I had quite forgotten our cover. I had become so absorbed in thinking of what lies ahead of us.'

'Well, we'll have to tell the landlord we are leaving tomorrow, will we not?'

Will picked up on the impatience in Armstrong's voice but was still thinking of the courage of the fishermen and their families and for the moment found it hard to concentrate on the matter at hand.

Armstrong sighed. 'How about we say we are to stay with friends on the island for a time while we look for a likely place to settle?'

'A capital notion, Sergeant. As long as no one probes too deeply about our mythical friends.'

'Have you a better idea?'

'No, not one, Sergeant. I am indebted to you for your quick thinking.'

After they had dined – on fish, once again – and retired to their none too clean room, Armstrong started to pace up and down. Will finally took notice.

'Are you going to tell me what ails you Sergeant?'

Armstrong grunted.

'Come on Duncan,' said Will, and Armstrong looked up, startled, unused to being called by his first name.

'Spit it out, man!'

Armstrong hesitated. Then he sat down on the one available chair and looked up at Will.

'For the life of me, sir, I cannot imagine how I can serve you in this venture. I could understand hardly any of the speech of those fishermen. I know they speak a particular patois but my understanding of French is at best limited. I will immediately be taken for the Scot that I am.'

Will frowned. 'That has been concerning me, too, but I venture to suggest that we can turn the situation to our advantage.'

'How is that, sir?'

'For a large part of our time, we shall, I hope, be conversing with those sympathetic to our mission and, in those circumstances, we simply explain that you have some understanding of the French language but do not speak it confidently.'

'And with others? With those who are our enemies?'

'Then we shall have to think on our feet and both of us may have to use disguise, pretence and subterfuge.'

'I've no trouble with that, sir. It's the talking that'll expose me.'

'Then do not talk.'

Armstrong raised his eyebrows.

Will continued, gesturing to Armstrong's empty sleeve. 'Anyone can see that you have met with an accident. I shall simply explain that when you lost your arm you also sustained a severe blow to the head and that your speech has been severely affected and you find it embarrassing to try and form words with strangers.'

Armstrong grunted. 'I can already see a flaw in that story, sir.'

'And what would that be?'

'Why, in God's name, would you choose a dumb cripple for a travelling companion?'

Will threw back his head and laughed and Armstrong's spirits rose. It was the first time that he had seen a glimpse of the Captain of old, carefree and fun loving, not worn down with grief and guilt as he had been of late.

'Why indeed?' said Will, still laughing as he clapped Armstrong on the back. 'No point in worrying too much about the future, eh Sergeant? We'll face it together. We are fleet of foot and quick witted. We've been in many scrapes before have we not?'

Armstrong grinned and suddenly his forebodings seemed less burdensome.

'That we have, sir!'

'And stop calling me sir or Captain. We must not reveal our military background to any enemy.'

'If I'm a dumb cripple I won't be speaking!'

Will chuckled. 'Nor you will.'

'But you will have to remember not to address me as Sergeant.'

'Ah yes. I must work on that.'

Both men went to their beds in a better frame of mind, their former camaraderie restored and with the promise of adventure ahead. Just as he was dropping off to sleep, Armstrong muttered something.

Will yawned. 'Something bothering you, Serg..., Armstrong?'

'Just the prospect of more travel over the sea.'

'Not far this time.'

'Why should I believe you. That's what you said when we embarked at Southampton for Jersey.'

***

Late in the afternoon of the next day they rendezvoused with one of the fishermen they had met the night before. He was a man of few words and Will did not attempt to distract him from his task which, in the gathering darkness with a bitter wind blowing, was not an easy one. Armstrong and Will sat together on the central thwart, clinging on to the plank beneath them or, on occasion, to the sides of the vessel. The wind had whipped up the waves and the spray covered them as they climbed one wave only to slide down the other side and face the next.

At last they anchored, not on the French coast but beside what seemed to be nothing more than a large rock looming up alongside them, a menacing presence in the darkness.

Will stretched his aching arms. 'Are we to be set down here? What is this place? I understood we were to land close to the fishing village you spoke of.'

Their companion was busy lowering the sails and did not immediately answer and for a moment Will wondered whether this whole business was a double bluff, that they were being delivered into the hands of their enemies, that the fisherman was not a royalist at all but a true supporter of Napoleon. It was obvious that Armstrong, too, was alarmed and he twisted on the seat to reach for his dagger.

But the fisherman, having loosed the sails, turned to explain.

'The Chausey islets,' he said.

Armstrong nudged Will. 'What's the fellow saying?'

'These are an uninhabited group of small islands,' he said. 'You remember the fishermen mentioned them last night - and I noted them on Reeves's map. They lie a little distance out to sea across from the town of Granville.'

'Why in heavens are we anchored here?'

Will shrugged, then spoke again to the fisherman asking that very question.

In answer, the man laughed softly. 'Did you think I would abandon you here? No man can live here, these islets are naught but rocks and sand but there are plenty of good hiding places above the tideline.'

'Ah! This then is where you pick up messages from the French royalists and leave letters for them?'

'Aye. We have a good system, a different place in a different islet each day. Our friend Gabriel devised it.'

'Then we won't delay you,' said Will.

The man jumped over the side of the boat and waded through the shallow water, carrying a leather pouch above his head and then they saw him walking up the tiny sandy cove and vanish round the side of the huge rock. He was not gone long and returned to the boat with another leather pouch. He dusted the sand from it and stowed it in the bulkhead, then he started to raise the sails again.

When they were once more on their way, Will asked him whether the pouches were hidden under the sand.

'Aye, we conceal them beneath the sand where only those who

46

know the exact hiding places will find them.'

'An ingenious plan. And you say no one comes to these islets.'

'None but us and our French royalist friends. The rocks beneath the surface of the sea here can be treacherous and there's no life here except the birds. It's no place to come if you don't understand the waters.'

Armstrong shuffled on his seat. 'Don't keep him talking sir. I warrant he'll need all his wits to get us clear of the rocks.'

Dawn was breaking as they sailed South, parallel to the French coast. Both Will and Armstrong kept silent, their thoughts full of the dangers that lay ahead of them.

It was only just light when their companion dropped them off at a remote bay.

'This is where we part,' he said. 'You have directions, yes? You know what to do?'

Will nodded and shook the man's hand briefly. 'We are indebted to you,' he said. 'I pray to God that we shall not let you down.'

The man didn't reply but immediately changed tack to head away from the coast after Will and Armstrong had grabbed their paltry possessions, scrambled over the side of the boat and waded ashore.

'No doubt he'd be apprehended if he was observed so close to French soil,' said Armstrong as they walked swiftly over the sand. The terrain was as had been described to them and they had no time for idle talk as they climbed upwards, over sharp outcrops of rock, onto the rough land beyond and headed with all speed to the forest ahead of them. It was only here, hidden by the trees, that they felt able to pause and take a drink from a rock-strewn stream that tumbled downwards between the trees. Both men were dressed in peasant's garb supplied to them by their Jersey comrades. They wore tunics and stockings under sheepskin cloaks and had woollen hats pulled down over their hair and mittens on their hands to protect them from the cold. They had walked barefoot from the sea but now they sat to pull on the short leather boots they'd been given. Armstrong was struggling to put his on and Will helped him. When he'd done so, he got to his feet and stood, arms folded, looking down on his Sergeant with amusement.

Armstrong's beard had grown wild and bushy and his face was none too clean nor were the garments they'd been given.

'You make a fine French peasant, Sergeant,' said Will.

Armstrong pushed himself upright. 'As do you, sir,' he grunted.

Then they both laughed. 'We *must* learn to drop the Sir and Sergeant,' said Will.

'Aye,' said Armstrong, squinting up at the sunlight which was coming through the trees and making the water in the stream sparkle. 'Do you reckon it's time to move?'

Will nodded. 'No doubt the market at Granville will open early. If we strike off through the forest we should meet the track that leads to the road into the town.'

As they came out of the trees they could see the road in the distance and they noted that there was already a straggle of people walking along it towards the town. Among the walkers there were horse drawn carts full of produce, beasts being driven forward by their owners and many people on foot, some carrying goods of one sort or another to sell, others unburdened.

They strolled along the track towards the road and as they drew closer, Will bent down and whispered 'Remember not to speak! And from now on I, too, shall only speak if absolutely necessary and then it will be in French. I have no doubt that there is a strong local accent and I shall do my best to copy it.'

Armstrong raised his eyebrows but said nothing and soon they found themselves among the throng moving along the road towards the town. One or two acknowledged their presence but most were concerned with their own business and Will was relieved to see that his dress, and that of the Sergeant, exactly echoed those of the other peasants and farmers.

Those Jersey royalists know their job.

Chapter Nine

When they finally reached Granville, they were shocked by the devasted buildings everywhere and it was only then that Will remembered hearing of the bombardment of the town by the Royal Navy in 1803, after the coast had been blockaded.

The market was already in full swing with stalls selling bread, turnips, pork and mutton, as well as locally made furniture, tools and garments. Will and Armstrong wandered among the stalls, even making a few small food purchases, eating as they walked, glad to fill their stomachs again. Armstrong was playing the dumb fellow with some skill and it was he who spotted the fish stall in the far corner of the market hard by the sale ring where animals were herded and, poking Will in the ribs, pointed to it.

Casually, they sauntered over to it, observing that there was a woman at the stall, serving customers, accompanied by a young man. They were both hard at work, the woman passing the time of day with a smile for everyone, deftly wrapping fish in muslin and handing it over while the young man at her side took payment. Will waited until the crush had eased then went up to the stall to enquire about the availability of smoked herring, slipping a coded phrase into the conversation as he did so.

The woman looked up briefly but betrayed nothing as she replied.

'No smoked herring today, sir, but I have some dried cod at the back of the stall if you would care to come this way. I think you will find it a fair substitute.'

It was all said so naturally that any casual observer would find nothing unusual in this exchange and as Will thanked the woman and followed her round to the back of the stall, he wondered at her boldness. In no time he found himself the recipient of some dried cod and a whispered instruction, then he paid the boy for the fish and walked away. He re-joined Armstrong who was gazing about him, his mouth gaping slightly and as they continued to pause at various stalls, Will could not but smile at his impersonation of an amiable idiot. He gestured for Armstrong to follow him and walked out of the town in the opposite direction from where they had come and did not stop until they were in sight of a fishing village along the coast to the North of Granville. When he was certain no one could observe them, Will slowed down and looked about him.

'The woman mentioned a broken down animal shelter somewhere here above the village,' he said, 'but I cannot see it.'

Armstrong frowned. 'I think I have it.' He pointed and, at first, Will could see nothing resembling a shelter.

'It is well hidden. There,' he pointed again. 'Behind that boulder.'

'Your eyes are sharper than mine, Ser... Duncan.'

They walked over to the shelter and then, turning once more to make sure they were not observed, slipped inside where they sat, their backs against the wooden wall where they were sheltered from the wind.

'So that was Pipette?' asked Armstrong.

Will nodded. 'She answered to the name of Pipette and replied correctly to the password I slipped into the conversation. She will come to us here at three after noon, when the market closes.'

'So we kick our heels here until then do we, sir?'

'Unless you have a better idea. We are out of sight and at least there is some shelter from the weather.'

As they finished their victuals they talked quietly among themselves. After a while, Armstrong stood up and stamped on the ground then walked up and down trying to get some feeling back into his numb feet.

'I hope she comes soon,' he said. 'We'll die of cold if we have to stay here much longer.'

Will put his finger to his lips. 'Hush! Listen!'

For now, in the distance, came the sound of talking and laughter from the direction of the town, then the sounds of feet tramping along the track. As the sounds grew louder, Armstrong grinned. 'Folk returning from the market, I'd wager, heading for their homes and warm fires.' He shivered. 'Lucky bastards.'

Will removed his gloves, rubbed his hands together and blew on them. As he replaced the gloves, he whispered.

'With luck, Pipette will be here before long, then. She indicated that she would need to pack up her stall but she'll want to be home before the light fades, no doubt.'

At length, the noise of laughter and chatter and the trundling of carts along the track faded away and there was silence again save for the relentless sound of the wind.

They waited and the light was fading fast.

'It must be well past three o'clock,' said Armstrong. 'Are we wise to rely upon her so utterly, sir?'

Will shrugged. 'What choice do we have?' He shifted his position to ease his aching joints. 'You heard what Florence told us while we were in Jersey. I am sure Pipette won't let us down.'

'Huh, you may have heard what she said, sir. I couldn't make head nor tail of it.'

'Patience, Sergeant.'

'Don't call me Sergeant!'

But when she did come, she took them both completely by surprise. They were listening out for the sound of a cart on the track as she brought her unsold produce back to the village, or voices as she spoke to the lad who had been helping her, or even a footfall or the crack of a broken twig but there was nothing. Instead, she was suddenly there, silent as the dead, slipping into the shelter, crowding in beside them.

'Madame!' whispered Will. 'You appeared from nowhere. You quite startled us.'

Pipette was a small woman and even in the gloom of the shelter, they could sense her alertness and quick movements. When he had spoken to her before, it had seemed to Will that she was of middle years and somewhat ponderous but he realised at once that this persona must be a deliberate ruse for, now when she spoke, her voice sounded younger.

'Ah sir, I am well used to slipping unseen in and out of hiding places, quiet as a mouse.'

She gave a quiet chuckle. 'It is a skill you would do well to develop if you are to succeed in your mission.'

'You know of …' began Armstrong, in his halting French.

'I received news of your arrival,' she said. 'We have an excellent

51

network as you have no doubt discovered and although that weasel Fouché seeks to destroy us, we are too clever for him. We move too quickly, open a new safe house as an old one closes, recruit more loyal royalists as others flee the country or are captured.

'A mighty dangerous business,' commented Will.

'And you, too, sir, have known danger.'

'Aye,' said Armstrong, in his stumbling French, 'We have, Madame. And have no fear of facing it again if we are serving our country.'

Will glanced at him and was relieved that he understood the woman whose speech was free of the confusing Jersey patois.

'However,' went on Pipette, 'Gaston was at the heart of the network. It was he who had made it what it is and now …' She hesitated and shrugged into the gloom. 'Now no one knows what has happened to him.'

'We heard that he was captured.'

'Only a rumour, sir, but it is likely.'

'Why do you think that, Madame?'

'Because he was constantly sending messages, passing on information. And now there is nothing. All communication from him has stopped.'

'Have you met him, Madame?'

'None here have met him. His identity is secret but we think he may be a diplomat as he has the ability to travel freely and seems to be able to gather information from outside the country.'

Will glanced briefly at Armstrong, who was examining his feet. *Even these loyal royalists do not know that Gaston is a woman.*

'Where do you advise we start our search, Madame. Where can we find out more about his whereabouts?'

'We think it likely that, if he is held captive, it would be somewhere near the capital.'

'Near Paris?'

'Fouché would undoubtedly want to keep him close, if, indeed, he has him.'

Pipette looked out at the darkening sky. 'We must hurry,' she said. 'I have arranged accommodation for you tonight with another fishing family and they will provide you with the address of the next safe house. And so on as you travel East.

'But surely,' said Armstrong, 'There are royalist agents nearer to Paris who can help Gaston escape?'

She shook her head. 'You do not understand. Fouché's men are everywhere seeking out cells of royalists. We cannot know how many he has identified and where he will strike next. But he will know nothing of you. And,' she added. 'I'm told you have been sent by your Government. You are privy to more information than any single agent has.'

Will stared at the small woman and wondered at her bravery. 'What about you, Madame? Are you not in grave danger?'

Pipette shrugged. 'All of the fishing community here are under suspicion since poor Gabriel was captured but they can prove nothing – at least not yet. We play the part of dumb peasants with no interest in politics and have them believe that only the Jersey fishermen were agents of the British and passing on information.'

Will smiled. There was nothing dumb about Pipette. As they had intimated to him in Jersey, she was as sharp as a dagger.

'Madame, I swear that we shall do our best to find this Gaston and bring him to safety,' said Will.'

'I believe that you have the advantage of knowing his identity?'

Neither Will nor Armstrong said anything.

'I have no desire to know it,' she added. Then she told them where to find the fishing family who would give them lodging and slipped quietly away.

When she had gone, Will turned to Armstrong. 'She's wrong about Fouché knowing nothing of us,' he said.

'What? How could he know of us?'

'Think back, Duncan. Have you so soon forgotten what happened when we were last on French soil? The traitor de Menou was blackmailing my brother's colleague James Montagu. James tricked me into leading him to Jack. James murdered Jack and then I killed James. And then De Menou fled back to France which indicates that he will have known all of this and certainly will have informed Fouché. Indeed, I suspect that all the time that de Menou was embedded in the British Government, calling himself Samuel Barker, he would have been in close touch with Fouché as a valued informant.'

'Christ,' said Armstrong. 'And there I was thinking we'd be travelling incognito.'

'De Menou may not know your name, Duncan, but he will certainly know mine. Which is why we must assume false ones.

'What? Now?'

'Yes. At once. You must think of me as Etienne.'

Armstrong frowned. 'Then I shall be Pierre, though as I'm supposed to be a dumb idiot I doubt that anyone will need to know my name.'

Will took Armstrong's good arm and they crept out of the shelter and back onto the track, then they made their way down to the fishing village and the house where they were to lodge.

'One good thing about this venture,' said Armstrong just before they reached the village.

'What is that?'

'We shall be on dry land at least.'

'Ah, but you are acclimatising to travel by water, Duncan, are you not? I observed that you were not once sick on our voyage over from Jersey.'

Armstrong grunted.

Chapter Ten

As they reached the village it was nearly dark and there were few people abroad but Pipette's instructions had been clear and they found the house with no trouble and were ushered inside with all haste. The family consisted of a man and his wife and several children, the eldest of whom, a girl, looked vaguely familiar to Will. As she served them with a simple meal of fish and rough bread, she smiled at him and he felt bold enough to ask if they had met before.

'I was at the stall in the market,' she said.

Will frowned. 'It was you, helping Pipette? But I thought ...'

Her mother interrupted. 'You thought she was a young man?' And when Will nodded, she laughed. 'Ah good!'

'We trust no-one,' said her father. 'Since so many royalist agents have been exposed, we use every disguise we can.' He glanced fondly at his daughter. 'It is safer for her to go abroad as a young man. All the locals know who she is but there are many visitors to the marketplace.'

Will didn't like to probe further while the children were around. He waited until their mother had shooed the younger ones up the cottage stairs, through the door alongside the large open fireplace. When she came down, she nodded at her older daughter who immediately went out to clean the dishes. Will felt bold enough then to ask how he and Armstrong might find transport to make their way towards the capital.

The woman shook her head. 'Pipette will come shortly. She has more knowledge; she only tells us what we need to know.' She looked across at her husband. 'It is safer that way.'

I wonder at their courage. If they were uncovered as royalist supporters, then they would lose everything.

It was not long before the back door opened softly and Pipette appeared. She beckoned Will and Armstrong into a tiny back parlour where, by the light of a single candle, she answered their questions as best she could, explaining how they would be transported from one safe house to the next on the long journey

East.'

'How far is it?' asked Armstrong, in his halting French.

'About 200 miles,' she said, then glancing at Will. 'Do not let your companion speak, sir. You speak the language well, though you must adjust to the local accent, but he will immediately be taken as a foreigner.'

'He will feign idiocy,' said Will. Armstrong scowled but said nothing.

'Be sure not to let your guard down.' She paused, looking at their rough peasant garb. 'Your Jersey friends have dressed you well but as you travel East you will need other disguises.'

'It seems you have a well organised network, Madame,' said Will.

Pipette sighed. 'Indeed, it was very well organised, but with these recent betrayals, we are having to adjust all the time. It seems that every day we have news of safe houses discovered and agents rounded up.' She looked down at her clasped hands, and even though the light was poor, Will could see the deep worry lines on her brow.

'You risk much, Madame. How long have you been helping ...?'

'Many along this coastline have been involved,' she said. Then she continued, sensing the unspoken question in Will's voice.

'You wonder why, sir?'

Will nodded.

'The Revolution was brutal,' she said. 'You may think that we simple fishing people were not affected but we found our menfolk taken away to fight, leaving none to man the boats and bring in the catch. For sure, the Ancien Régime had many faults but we had an ordered life and as for the Godlessness of the Revolution!' She raised her eyes to the ceiling. 'Churches were closed, worship banned.'

'I sense that you are a woman of faith?'

'You do not battle with the wind and tides without having respect for God,' she said quietly.

'And now, Madame,' asked Will. 'Are things better?'

She nodded. 'We are free to worship, at least, but these wars! All my life, our country has been at war and now this madman wants to conquer the world, it seems. The country is impoverished. We need peace so that we can all prosper.'

Will nodded and, if he was surprised at the strength of Pipette's words, he did not show it.

We have been fighting against the French for so long, but what do we know of the feelings of the ordinary people of the country? I have always seen the whole nation as a force to be defeated and given little thought to those who have had their livelihoods disrupted.

He glanced at Armstrong and sensed that he, too, was thinking along the same lines. They had assumed that, once she had given them their instructions, Pipette would take her leave but she showed no sign of going and a little later they were joined in the parlour by their hosts when they discussed, with more freedom, how the royalist cause had been helped by people living in these coastal villages in Normandy.

'1804 was a bad year,' said Pipette, and the others nodded. 'That was when Napoleon's headquarters were just south of Boulogne.'

The husband cleared his throat. 'So many royalist agents were uncovered then and more and more troops and naval workers came. Everyone was watched.'

'That year, deliveries for our agents started to go through Le Tréport, further South,' continued the man, and that worked well.' He chuckled. 'The schoolmaster there was responsible for naval signals and he sold them to the royalists so the British ships knew the correct signals and could pass as friendly vessels.'

'Hush man,' said his wife. 'You must not reveal all these secrets. It is not wise for our British friends to know too much.' But she was smiling as she spoke.

Pipette got up to take her leave. 'It is late,' she said, 'And you must be tired.

Will rose to his feet, knocking his head on a ceiling beam as he did so. 'We are indebted to you, Madame,' he said.

Pipette moved out into the kitchen. As she reached the outside door she turned back. 'Can I leave you to check the oyster shed,' she said quietly, addressing the couple.

'Of course.'

Armstrong was frowning. He whispered to Will, 'They have to go and check on the oysters at this time of night!'

Their hostess caught the drift of his remark. 'On market days we sometimes have a drop off late at night.'

'A drop off?'

She looked across at her husband. 'Information comes to us from many quarters,' he said. 'We have a place of concealment in the oyster sheds.'

The man got up and stretched. "I'll go,' he said, touching his wife's shoulder as he passed her. Then, nodding towards Will and Armstrong. 'If there is any news which may affect you, I will tell you in the morning.'

They all followed him through into the kitchen where he took his coat from a peg in the wall, shrugged it on and then pulled a woollen hat down over his head. His wife lit a lantern and handed it to him. He shaded the light with his hand as he left, letting a blast of icy wind into the room before closing the door quietly behind him. She gazed at the closed door for a moment, sighed and then busied herself preparing a place for Will and Armstrong to sleep, dragging a couple of rough pallets from out of a cupboard and lying them in front of the inglenook fireplace. Then she went to a chest in the corner of the room and took out some loosely woven blankets.

'This stone floor is mighty hard, sirs,' she says. 'I hope you will not be too uncomfortable.'

'We are very grateful, Madame, said Will.' He gestured to the bedding. 'And we have slept in much rougher beds than these.' Armstrong sensed that Will was about to refer to their life in the army and shot him a warning glance. 'We should not give away our background,' he whispered in English. Will frowned but said no more. After the woman had banked up the fire and gone up the stairs to the floor above, he turned to Armstrong.

'Surely we can trust these people Duncan?'

Armstrong shrugged. 'Can't be too careful sir … I mean Etienne.'

Will grinned. 'Etienne. I like the name. And I must remember to refer to you as Pierre. But why should we not explain our background?'

'No need to, is there? If it got about that we are fighting men, it might reach other ears, perhaps.'

'Ah. I catch your drift. Yes. We could put these kind people in a difficult position. What they don't know, they cannot reveal if ...'

'If they are questioned,' finished Armstrong.

They looked at each other and, of a sudden, Will gave an involuntary shiver despite the warmth of the room.

The next morning they were awakened very early, before dawn. Someone was shaking Will's shoulder and he sat up, at once alert, to see their host squatting down beside him.

'You must leave now, sir,' he whispered.

Will staggered to his feet. 'Has something happened,' he asked as he groped for his overgarments which he had laid on the wooden chest.

The man nodded. 'We had a warning last night,' he said.

'A warning?'

'When I went to the oyster sheds, I found a note. 'There are soldiers on their way to search our village.'

'Why did you not tell us this last night?' said Will.

'I went first to Pipette with the news and by the time I came back here you and your companion were asleep. We thought it better to let you rest, but Pipette has made all the arrangements for your departure and my wife has some victuals for your journey. There is a cart outside. I beg you sir, leave with all haste.'

By this time, Armstrong was awake and sitting up, rubbing his eyes.

'We leave immediately, Pierre,' said Will, the name not coming easily to his lips. Armstrong heard the urgency in his voice and didn't question the order but was on his feet in seconds and putting on his outer clothes as Will helped him with his boots.

'From which direction will the soldiers come?' asked Will as he took the bundle of food the woman gave him.

'From Granville. But you will be travelling East. As long as you go now you should be safe. There are tracks through the forest inland and I doubt the soldiers will be here at the village before you are gone. But I beg you to hurry.'

Will and Armstrong hardly had time to give the couple their thanks and bid them farewell before they were out into the freezing morning and climbing up into a high sided farm cart where they concealed themselves beneath piles of loose hay. The driver of the cart piled more hay on top of them and then put a covering over that, fastening it with bindings under the cart. This was all done in silence and with speed and skill in the pre-dawn darkness and in no time they were on their way, a sturdy carthorse between the shafts pulling them up from the coast and along the track they had travelled the day before.

'It's fearsome uncomfortable here,' whispered Armstrong. 'Where do you suppose we are being taken?'

Will's eyes were smarting and he was trying to suppress a sneeze. 'Just keep quiet. The driver is risking much doing this for us.'

They had been going a while when the horse began to pick up speed and they sensed that dawn had broken and the way ahead was clearer. Will shuffled to the side and lifted the edge of the covering to peer out. 'We are just entering the forest,' he said. 'Once on the track here, we should be out of the way of prying eyes.'

'Thank God for that,' said Armstrong, moving forward awkwardly to join him and finding another loose flap of covering to lift up.

'We should unwrap these victuals and see what our friend has given us to eat,' said Will, suddenly feeling ravenously hungry.

'Aye, I could fancy ....' But Armstrong didn't finish the sentence. Instead, he moved back into the body of the cart with all speed and yanked Will's collar, gesturing for him to do the same.'

'What...?'

'Bastards!' he whispered.

'What?'

'Just caught a glimpse of them, the sneaky buggers.'

Armstrong couldn't see Will's face but sensed his puzzlement.

'Soldiers, sir!'

'Are you sure?'

'Think I don't know a soldier when I see one? They're making ready to go down into the village.'

Will wanted to take another look but he restrained himself.

'They must have made a great circuit round the village and come into the forest from the other way then concealed themselves among the trees overnight ready for a dawn raid.'

'Just as well our friend went to the oyster sheds last night,' said Will grimly.

The horse plodded on along the track through the forest.

'Should we warn the driver?' whispered Armstrong.

'Can't do that without revealing ourselves. We'll just have to hope he holds his nerve if they stop him.'

'How many do you reckon there are?'

'Too many for us to take on my friend.'

'Aye.'

Still the horse plodded on, its pace unaltered. Will's whole body itched and his eyes watered. Both men lay still, bodies tensed, waiting. The only sound the regular thud thud of the hooves accompanied by an occasional snort from the horse and, very faintly, the beginning of the muted birdsong of a winter dawn.

And then, suddenly, a loud voice 'Halt!' and a violent jerk of the cart and a shifting of the load of hay as the horse was reined in.

Then another voice. And another. It seemed that there was a group of soldiers surrounding the cart. From their hiding place, deep in the hay, Will and Armstrong had difficulty in making out the words exchanged with the driver though one phrase came out clearly: 'Where are you going and what's your business?'

There was a quieter voice then, that they could only assume was the voice of the driver and then the tone of the soldiers' voices changed, becoming less aggressive, more friendly. Will caught one or two words: '…pretty lass like you … your uncle's farm you say … better do our duty and search the hay.' …. Followed by more laughter and the unmistakable sound of swords being unsheathed.

It took all their willpower to keep from shrinking further back but any movement would surely be noticed so they waited, hardly daring to breathe, as the covering was untied and they saw sword blades being plunged through the hay towards them. One grazed

Will's leg but he managed to force himself to keep still, his eyes closed. Then he saw another jabbing at the place where Armstrong lay. Armstrong bit down on his lip, waiting for an impact and Will watched, horrified, as a blade drew blood as it sliced his ear. But Armstrong kept silent, only his eyes screwing up in pain.

There were a few, somewhat half-hearted thrusts into the hay but mercifully none that struck home and at last, with more lewd remarks and laughter, the soldiers retied the covering and the cart started to move forward again. The men lay in silence until the voices had faded into the distance.

'Christ, sir, that was close,' whispered Armstrong.

Will shifted nearer. 'Are you hurt?'

'Damn Frenchie took off a bit of my ear, that's all. It's bleeding like a stuck pig but there's no real harm done.'

'We may not be so lucky if it happens again.'

'Surely they'll be off down to the village now?'

Will shifted and then sneezed as dust from the hay got up his nose though he managed to silence the noise quickly.

'As well you didn't do that just now.'

'Aye.'

They were silent then, as their journey continued, the horse pulling them steadily along the track. After a while, they unwrapped their victuals and ate hungrily the bread and salted herring provided, though as they did so they disturbed more dust and Armstrong had to smother a cough. They had left the village in such haste that they'd had no time to fill their water bottles and both men were parched.

'You still got your pocket watch sir,' asked Armstrong, after a while.

'No I left it in London.'

'Pity. It would be good to know the time.'

'Aye, but no peasant would own one, would they? If one was discovered on my person I'd be outed as a thief, I reckon.'

Armstrong grunted. 'Or an officer.'

It was late in the morning when, at last, the cart came to a standstill. The men stayed where they were and waited until, at length, the covering was untied and the driver spoke quietly to them.

'We are at a farm, sirs and inside a barn. You can come out safely now.'

Stiffly, they descended from the cart, pulling wisps of hay from their hair and their clothing, and looked about them. In the gloom of the barn it took them a moment to recognise their young driver, the daughter of last night's hosts who had been helping Pipette at the market the day before, dressed as a young man.

'Ye gods!' exclaimed Will, 'It is you!'

The young woman smiled at him.

'Forgive me Mademoiselle,' said Will. 'I am so shocked that my manners have deserted me. You are a brave young woman and we are in your debt.'

'I was frightened when those soldiers surrounded me,' she said, 'and very alarmed when they started pushing their swords into the hay.'

'What story did you tell them?' asked Will.

'It was mostly the truth, I said that my uncle's farm had had a poor hay harvest and he had run short and that I was bringing him supplies from elsewhere.'

'But your people are not farmers.'

She grinned. 'No, and this is not my uncle's farm, but the farmer here is a royalist and he will give you shelter.'

Chapter Eleven

Their arrival had been noted and they were soon joined by the farmer and, with Will's help, and that of their young driver, they unloaded the hay and stored it in the loft, scrambling up and down a wooden ladder to deposit the loose bundles. Armstrong stood at the base of the ladder to hold it steady, aware that with only one arm, that was the most useful job he could do.

At length, the farmer led them into his house and gave them much needed refreshment before their young driver set off again with an empty cart to drive back to the coast before sunset.

As they watched her heading back to the barn, Armstrong looked at her retreating figure.

'A brave young woman.'

The farmer looked at him. 'Be careful not to speak when you converse with those not friendly to our cause,' he said.

Will nodded. 'My friend Pierre is to present as a mute in those circumstances,' he said.

'Pierre?'

'Not his real name,' said Will.

'And I warrant your real name is not Etienne?'

'No. We have been advised not to reveal our real names.'

The farmer nodded. 'You have been well briefed.'

Later, when the rest of the household had retired, Will questioned the farmer closely as to what might be happening in the fishing village.

'Are those soldiers associated with Fouché's men?' he asked.

The man shrugged. 'They will have their orders,' he said. 'Fouché controls the secret police in Paris. He will need their support to seek out and arrest any who oppose the regime in this region.'

'And will they be successful?'

'All along this coast royalist agents come and go and smugglers trade in contraband. Raids are not uncommon.'

Will wondered how much he should tell this man about his mission. He moved his chair closer. 'I was informed that many of our agents have been betrayed recently.'

The farmer looked up sharply. 'I, too, have heard that. I understand that there was a traitor in your Government who was acting as a double agent and was privy to the identity of many of your agents.'

Will nodded. 'Then I can speak freely?'

'Of course.'

'Have you heard of an agent called Gaston?'

The farmer looked up then and met Will's eyes. 'I know the name, sir. Do you have some business with him?'

'It is our belief,' said Will, choosing his words carefully, 'that he may have been captured.'

The man showed no surprise. 'If he was running agents then that is hardly surprising.'

'Sir, may I ask if you were …?'

'No.' He shook his head. 'I am not part of a network. I have …' He shuffled in his seat. 'I am not allied to anyone but I do favours for friends from time to time by giving shelter to those they send me.'

'And easing their passage across the channel, perhaps?'

'I occasionally have a word.'

'And you ask no questions?'

'What I do not know, I cannot reveal,' he said shortly.

Will rubbed his chin. A beard was beginning to grow which suited his disguise as a peasant.

'And your workers on the farm? Are they of your persuasion?'

Will saw a flash of anger in the man's eyes. 'Only family members work my land,' he said. 'And they have good reason for being bitter towards Napoleon's rule.'

'Your family have been …?'

'You ask too many questions, my friend. You do not need to know my business and I will ask no questions of yours.'

'Apologies, sir, I did not mean to offend.'

There was a long silence before Will spoke again.

'However, I would like to tell you my business. We have been tasked with helping …'

'We?' The farmer gestured to Armstrong who was sitting by the fire some distance from them. 'But how can he help if he is posing as mute and does not speak the language?'

Will glanced at Armstrong and saw that he had understood the farmer's words.

'My friend is an excellent observer,' he said, somewhat tartly. 'And he understands more than you may think. He is also a mean fighter.'

The farmer looked at Armstrong's empty sleeve and raised an eyebrow.

'We have been tasked with helping those agents who have been exposed,' continued Will, briskly. 'We are given to understand that many of them have fled their homes and are seeking sanctuary in England.'

The man nodded. 'And you are about to ask me if I would give them shelter and arrange a safe crossing should they seek me out?'

'I imagine it is too much to ask?'

To Will's surprise, the man suddenly laughed.

'I am delighted!' he said, rubbing his hands together. 'Delighted that the English know nothing of me!'

Will frowned. 'Sir,' he began.

'It means, my friend, that I am not suspected. Not suspected by the regime here and my name is not known by the English spy network.'

'I am truly glad to hear that sir. Does this mean that you will agree to …?'

The farmer stood up and stretched. 'I am already doing it my friend, as are several others, but we are doing so privately, unknown to those who organise the network agents.'

'Then how do those fleeing know of you?'

'I cannot reveal that.'

There was another silence while Will absorbed this information.

'I respect that you will not reveal your methods, sir, and I, too, am delighted that you have not fallen under suspicion.'

'It is because my routine has never changed. I, or one of my sons, drive to market each week in the next town East, which we have been doing for years, and I supply a particular household with certain produce, which, again, I have been doing for years. You do not need to know how the information is passed, but at the end of market day there are certain exchanges in the tavern where we slake our thirst after a long day before driving back.'

'And that is how these refugees come to your door?'

'Indeed.'

'And no one else knows of this arrangement?'

'Pipette is aware and is utterly to be trusted, but she knows I do not wish it to become known among royalist agents that I give shelter to those fleeing. She does not know the name of my contact in the next town and he has not revealed to me his contact further up the chain. So far this has worked in our favour.'

'What you do not know, you cannot reveal,' repeated Will softly.

'Indeed.'

'You will be taken to my contact in the next town, but not until market day. Until then, you must hide here. Now, sir, you have had a long day and I'll warrant you are ready for your bed. All is prepared for you in an attic and I will ask you to stay in the house and not go outside unless I direct you to do so.'

Will nodded. 'Of course, sir. And let me repeat how grateful ...'

The man dismissed his thanks with a wave of his hand, and as he was showing Will and Armstrong up to their room, he said, before leaving them. 'My contact in the next town is a man of learning and travels to Paris from time to time. I am a simple farmer but he has a wide circle of friends and he may be able to give you more information.'

Will and Armstrong stayed several days with the farmer. They saw no one except his sons and his wife, none of whom showed any surprise at their presence and nor did they question them.

They heard news from the village that, although the soldiers had caused havoc and fear among the people there, they had found no evidence of fleeing royalists and had finally left calling out curses and threats to return.

'Pipette's quick thinking saved us a deal of trouble,' said Armstrong. 'If the soldiers had found us then ...'

'Then our mission would have ended before it began,' finished Will.

At last the day came when they were to leave for the next town

Eastwards.

This time they were concealed in a false compartment in a large cart. The cart was filled with a range of goods, from turnips, parsnips, swedes and celeriac set in trays to preserve them, together with a variety of farm implements and leather goods. One of the farmer's sons was a smith and repaired farm implements and the other had a side line in leather repair, so there was also a heap of bridles, straps, head collars and even a couple of saddles piled up. As Will and Armstrong crawled into the cavity where they were to hide, Armstrong remarked, 'If we are to travel all the way to Paris in this way, the journey will never end.'

The farmer overheard. 'Once you are away from here, your journey will be quicker, I assure you.' Then he slapped the carthorse on its rump and signalled to his son to drive off.

They had set off just after dawn and it was still early in the morning when they reached their destination. Following their instructions, they stayed concealed while the goods were unloaded, then they felt movement again as the cart moved off. When it came to a halt, the farmer's son unlatched the false compartment and they crawled out stiffly and saw that they were in a small barn.

'Stay here,' whispered the farmer's son. 'Your contact will be here soon.' He gestured to a dark corner of the barn where there was some sacking hanging from a beam.

'Conceal yourselves there,' he said. Then, as Will and Armstrong shuffled towards the end of the barn, he attached a nosebag to the horse's head and wishing them good luck, slipped away to man the stall in the market.

They crouched there behind the sacking for some time, Armstrong becoming more and more restless. At first Will was short tempered with him, telling him to be patient, but as the minutes went by, he, too, became anxious and, although he did not voice his opinion, he was beginning to wonder whether someone would, indeed, come to them and if they did not, what they should do next.

At least an hour had passed and he was beginning to form an alternative plan and was sharing his thoughts with Armstrong when, suddenly, they stiffened. There was a slight noise ahead of them, where the horse and cart stood, and the sound of humming.

Although they couldn't make out each other's expressions in the darkness, Will could sense Armstrong feeling for his dagger. Then they heard someone speaking softly to the horse and patting it.

'What a good fellow you are, to be sure.'

It was a man's voice, not with the strong accent of the farmer and the fishing community. It was a cultured voice.

Will and Armstrong didn't move but listened intently and it was only when the stranger had repeated his words to the horse several times, patting the beast in between times, that Armstrong nudged Will.

'That phrase in the middle. The words are in English,' he whispered.

Chapter Twelve

They listened again and, sure enough, the reassuring words were repeated, ostensibly to the horse, but with a phrase vilifying Napoleon, in English, interjected into the sentence each time.

Very cautiously, Will emerged from their hiding place. The inside of the barn was dark and he couldn't make out the man's features but he could see that he was wearing the garb of a priest.

As Will took a step forward, the man turned to him, expectantly, calmly, and folded his arms. He showed no fear or surprise.

For a few seconds, Will's brain could not engage and process what he was seeing.

Surely a man of God would not defy the regime? Is this some kind of trick?

Then he searched his mind for a suitable reply. The passwords they had memorised would not suffice as the farmer had told him that this man was not an official agent.

Fortunately, Armstrong was not so tongue tied. He came out of hiding then, and repeated the English phrase.

There was silence for a moment, then the man came forward.

'Father Jacques,' he said, extending his hand.

Will came out of his trance. 'My name is Etienne, Father' he said. 'And my companion is Pierre.'

'Not your real names, I assume?'

'You assume correctly.'

It was only then that they noticed that the priest was holding a sack. He put it down on the ground and proceeded to pull some garments from it. Then he held out to them two long black cassocks.

'I had to guess at the size,' he said. 'But I fancy these will fit.'

Armstrong gaped at him. 'Are you asking us to disguise ourselves as priests?'

Father Jacques laughed softly. 'You will find,' he said quietly, 'that people seldom give priests a second glance in this country. It is very convenient.'

Will was about to say more but the priest held up his hand. 'I would ask you to change with all haste,' he said, 'and put your own garments in this sack. My carriage is waiting a little distance away.'

Once they had changed, they followed him out of the barn, blinking in the daylight. As they emerged, Father Jacques addressed them. 'Remember, you are my students. I would ask you to show humility and follow behind me.' He gave a quiet chuckle. 'And if you lower your eyes to the ground and clasp your hands behind your backs, that will give an excellent impression of priestly obedience.'

'I cannot clasp my hands,' muttered Armstrong. 'And I cannot believe I would ever be taken for a priest. How will I explain the loss of my arm?''

'Even priests have accidents,' said Will.

Father Jacques was right. As the solemn little party progressed through the streets of the town, no one gave them a second glance. Occasionally, the Father would stop to give his blessing to a child or engage in conversation with one of his parishioners, but no one questioned the presence of the two young priestly students following at a respectful distance behind him.

His carriage was parked under a tree on the edge of the town, the horse's reins being held by another priest, who leapt up from his perch on a low wall as they approached. Father Jacques tapped the young man on the shoulder and bade him take the driver's seat, then he, together with Will and Armstrong, climbed inside the carriage. Once seated, he drew the curtains.

'We shall make our short journey away from the sun's glare,' he said.

Armstrong glanced across at Will. It was a damp, foggy, January day. However, they soon realised why Father Jacques wanted privacy.

'I am taking you to my house,' he said, 'And although I take every precaution and to my knowledge, I am still above suspicion, I would ask you to act the part of scholarly and respectful students when you reach it.'

'Of course, sir,' said Will. Armstrong grunted.

'And if I am to help you,' continued the priest, 'then I must know a little more about your mission.'

And so, as the carriage took them out of the town, away from the hustle and bustle of market day, Will answered the priest's questions in a general way.

Can I trust this man? My trust was betrayed before.

He had been speaking for a few minutes before Father Jacques held up his hand. 'My son, I feel that you are not being entirely frank with me.'

Will sighed. 'I'm sure you understand that I have to tread carefully, Father.'

There were a few moments silence, then Father Jacques spoke again. 'I know that Vicomte de Menou was a double agent,' he said. 'A traitor to our cause. I am also aware of the head of the royalist network, Gaston.'

'Even though you are not one of his agents?'

How much does he know of Gaston?

'Even so.' He hesitated and said, more quietly. 'There is much revealed to a priest in a confession.'

'Forgive me, Father. I was cruelly deceived on a previous mission and unwittingly led a murderer to his victim.' Will closed his eyes and fought back a wave of emotion as he remembered leading Montagu to find Jack.

'Ah. Then I can understand your caution, my friend.' He leant forward in his seat. 'Perhaps if I tell you a little about myself you will feel more comfortable confiding in me.'

He then proceeded to tell them of his own background, from a devout and wealthy family, and of the dechristianisation of France during the Revolution. He told them of the mass drownings of priests and nuns at Lyons, on the orders of Joseph Fouché, of the looting of churches and of the forced confiscation of lands owned by the church.

'That man again,' muttered Armstrong, hearing Fouché's name.

'Indeed,' said Father Jacques. 'He was powerful during the terror and even mention of his name struck fear into those of us in the service of the church.'

'And it seems he is still powerful,' said Will.

'Indeed. And it is only a few years since the Concordat was

signed by Napoleon in 1802.'

'The Concordat?'

'Between Napoleon and the church in Rome and France, defining the church's role here.'

'So the church has regained its status?'

Father Jacques sighed. 'To an extent but, as you can imagine, those who serve the church still remember Fouché's vicious attacks during the terror. He knows that many of us have royalist sympathies and the man's determination to hunt down and destroy any royalist cells in the country is undiminished.'

Will looked across at Armstrong. 'Hearing Father Jacques' story, Duncan,' he said in English, 'I am minded to trust him with ours.'

Armstrong nodded. 'I followed most of it. And I think you are right.' Then he grinned. 'And remember that my name is Pierre.'

Will cleared his throat. 'We have been sent by the British Government,' he said quietly. 'And our mission here is to help effect the escape of any royalist agents who are known to Fouché and his men and also to establish the whereabouts of Gaston and, if he is being held against his will, to try and free him.'

'A mighty task indeed,' muttered Father Jacques. 'I can certainly help you with the first. No one except Pipette and our farmer friend knows of my involvement in helping the royalists. I instruct young men who wish to enter the priesthood and there are always some at my house where they stay on retreat for a while and examine their consciences and decide whether they have a genuine calling. None are there for long, and this suits our cause. We also have visiting clergy passing through, some to lecture them, some simply to rest. So there is a constant stream of people coming and going. Your presence will not be remarked upon. You will be hiding in plain sight.'

'And you say you can help us?'

'Pipette has confided in me. She knows I will not betray her trust. She has revealed to me the names of certain people wanted by Fouché's men and who are still at large. I can give you this information and if you are able, you can send them here if you judge it wise, but they must be totally discreet, for obvious reasons. If I am suspected, then many people will suffer.' Then he frowned. 'You know that Napoleon has recently returned to the capital?'

'I know of his defeat of our forces at La Coruña and of the death of Sir John Moore. Has he returned to Paris to boast of his victory?'

Father Jacques shrugged. 'There are many reasons why he needs to return,' he said. 'But when he is in the country, there are always those plotting his death.'

Armstrong sat up. 'Are you saying that his life is in danger?'

'There have been many attempts at assassination.'

'I know of the one in 1800,' said Will.

'Ah yes, the famous one in rue Saint-Nicaise, funded by your Government.'

'And so nearly successful.'

Father Jacques looked up. 'A pity so many innocent bystanders were killed,' he said drily.

'And there have been others?' asked Armstrong.

'Several others. So, the Chief of Police is always on high alert when Napoleon is in the capital. He will redouble his efforts to find enemies of the regime. Any suspected of royalist tendencies are likely to be rounded up.'

'So we shall have to be extra vigilant?'

'Of course.'

There was silence in the carriage, the only sound, now they had left the town, was of the creaking wheels and of the horse's hooves as it trotted along the track.

'So you cannot help us as to the likely whereabouts of Gaston?'

'No. Though, if Fouché has him, he is likely to be confined somewhere near the capital.'

The carriage started to slow down and Father Jacques drew back the curtains. 'We are approaching my house,' he said.

Will and Armstrong peered out of the windows and saw that they were passing through some fine iron gates with a long driveway ahead. Then a large country house came into view and the carriage drew up in front of the main entrance.

'This is a mighty fine place,' said Armstrong.

74

'You are thinking that this is too fine for a man of God, my friend?'

'No. I was a little … surprised, sir. That is all.'

Father Jacques opened the door of the carriage and began to step down. Then he turned back. 'It belonged to my family,' he said. 'I was lucky that it was not confiscated during the Revolution.'

As Will and Armstrong descended from the carriage they were struck by the calmness and beauty of the place. The house was large and turreted and the gardens well-tended. There were formal beds either side of the entrance, though dormant and bereft of flowers at this time of year. The driveway behind them was lined with poplars which must give a fine show when in leaf. Beyond the lawns at the back were woods leading into the distance.

Inside the house there was, again, an atmosphere of calm. There were people about, many in black cassocks, but although they silently acknowledged Will and Armstrong with a smile or a nod, having done so they moved away going purposefully about their business.

'You have many people here, Father,' said Will.

He smiled. 'And all are assigned a job when they arrive. It is part of the priestly discipline that I impose on my students and, indeed, on others who visit and work here.' Then, as he led them into a large reception room on the ground floor, he added, 'Another discipline I impose on my visitors is not to ask personal questions of others but rather to contemplate and pray and to contribute whatever talents they may have to the common good.'

'I hope you will put us to work then, Father.'

'Indeed I shall.'

Will looked round the well appointed reception room which seemed strangely familiar to him in its furnishings. He glanced at Armstrong. 'Does this room remind you of another?'

Armstrong nodded. 'That traitor Montagu,' he whispered. 'His fancy house in London had similar furnishings, did it not?'

Will thought back to that fateful meeting with Montagu, in a room so tastefully furnished with French hangings and ornaments and furniture. A meeting at which he had been duped to become a decoy for Montagu's ends, to lead him to Jack. He shook his head to clear it of the unwelcome thoughts. Armstrong had seen his expression and nudged him.

'No good to dwell on the past, sir,' he said quietly.

Will nodded. 'You're right serg... Pierre. We have a mighty job ahead of us and we must concentrate all our energies on that.'

Father Jacques bid them sit down and for a few minutes he outlined his plans for them.

'We are short handed in the kitchen,' he said. 'So you will be put to work there.'

Will interrupted. 'We can do menial jobs, Father, but neither of us has culinary skills.'

'There are plenty of menial jobs you can do, my friends and it will only be for a day or so until I can arrange your onward journey.' He walked over to the fireplace and warmed his hands in front of the fire. 'As it happens, I am planning to make the journey to Paris very soon. There are colleagues I need to see there and people I need to bring back here.'

'To safety?' asked Will.

Father Jacques gave a slight nod but said nothing more. Then he summoned a servant to show them where they should sleep and what tasks could be allotted to them in the kitchen. As they were leaving the room, Armstrong turned back.

'The more we are delayed, Father, the more the danger increases for those ...'

Father Jacques held up his hand. 'I am well aware of that. Arrangements will be made with all possible speed, I assure you,' he said.

In the kitchen they were greeted warmly and set to work, Will chopping root vegetables for a huge stew of some sort and Armstrong mopping floors, at which he proved surprisingly adept despite his lack of an arm. As Father Jacques had intimated, they were not questioned, although Will thought that it must be obvious to the students of theology that they were misfits.

At one point, when Will had excused himself to visit the privy outside in the yard, he heard the sound of a high pitched laugh coming from somewhere nearby and then, as he headed back towards the house, he almost collided with a woman in a riding habit as she ran out of the stables, glancing back and calling to someone there.

'Excuse me, Madame,' said Will, stepping quickly out of her way.

She grabbed onto his arm to steady herself. 'Oh dear, sir, my apologies. It is entirely my fault. I wasn't looking where I was going.'

The hood had fallen back from her head and as she smiled up at him, Will was disarmed. She was a beauty. Tall and slim, her cheeks warmed by the wind and her eyes dancing with amusement, she observed him with unnerving candour.

'A new recruit,' she said. 'Have you recently arrived?'

'Just this afternoon,' said Will, bowing. 'And may I know your name Madame?'

'Blanche.'

'Blanche?'

She tapped her riding crop against her side. 'My surname is of no importance. And your name is?'

'Etienne,' said Will, remembering just in time.

'Not studying for the priesthood, I'd wager.'

'I …,' began Will, searching for words.

'Don't look so alarmed,' she said. 'Jacques has many visitors but you look to me more like a soldier than a priest.'

Will blushed.

Is it still obvious? She has seen me for what I am? My God, she's attractive!

'Father Jacques has been very kind and hospitable,' he said, knowing that he sounded ridiculously stiff and formal.

She laughed again. 'He is a charming man,' she said. She paused and, looking at him again, raising an eyebrow. 'As are you.' Then she was gone, running over the cobbled yard and round the side of the house.

His hopeless yearning for Clara aside, it was a long time since Will had been so instantly attracted to a woman. Not, indeed, since the unfortunate encounter in the Peninsular which had contributed to his disgrace.

Where does she fit into the household? She is clearly not a servant. What is her role here?

He was frowning as he made his way back into the kitchen to continue with his tasks but during the next hour or so the woman's face kept coming into his mind.

The rest of the day passed uneventfully. There was an ordered rhythm to the life of the house and after an evening meal the whole household gathered for prayers. With his head bowed, as were all the others, Will glanced around the sea of black robed men who surrounded him but there was no sign of the woman.

Chapter Thirteen

Although Will was exhausted, sleep would not come and he tossed and turned in his bed and listened to Armstrong's loud snores reverberating in the silence. At last, he got up and went out onto the landing outside, leaning over a balcony which overlooked the entrance hall of the house and thinking of what lay ahead.

Even if we make it to Paris safely, what then? If no one knows the whereabouts of this Gaston, then how can we find it out? And if Fouché has her then she will be heavily guarded. What happens to captured royalists?

He shivered, imagining hideous scenes of suffering at the hands of the Chief of Police.

They are unlikely to be treated as soldiers are treated when captured. They will not be considered as prisoners of war. And Gaston is a woman! What humiliation will be visited on her?

He stood there for a while knowing that Reeves had taken a risk in revealing her sex to him and Armstrong.

Neither Pipette nor Father Jacques seems to know she is a woman. We must keep this knowledge close.

He stood there for a while, turning over events in his mind and trying to think of strategies to use in the days and weeks ahead. They must be very careful when they reached the capital for it was here where they could make mistakes, be discovered as British agents, even fall into the hands of Fouché's men themselves. He and his brother Jack had visited Paris some years ago, but he did not know it well and he and Armstrong would have to move about the city unremarked.

He sighed and stretched his arms above his head and, just as he was about to turn and go back to his bed, he suddenly heard a sound coming from one of the chambers above him. He frowned and listened intently. Though the words were muffled, it was the unmistakable sound of a woman's voice, speaking in low tones and being answered by a man. A giggle, at once smothered, then a fond reprimand followed by more words in a man's voice.

As Will listened, he knew instinctively what he was hearing, though, in this house of priests, it seemed astonishing.

Somewhere, not far away from him, a man and a woman were making love.

His mind immediately went back to his encounter with the beautiful woman he had seen coming from the stables and her remark 'He is a charming man' when referring to Father Jacques.

His first emotion was that of jealousy. She was a stunningly attractive woman and in other circumstances …. But he knew, now, that he could not indulge such fantasies. He had no doubt that she was taken and that she was the mistress of Father Jacques.

Back in his bed, he considered the situation. Jacques was a good-looking man and he was clearly taking risks by harbouring him and Armstrong and, indeed, royalist refugees. Perhaps it was not so surprising that he took risks in other areas of his life. He was not a man who played by the rules. Will smiled, turned over and, putting a pillow over his head to try and drown out Armstrong's snores, he eventually dropped off to sleep.

The next day, there was no sign of Father Jacques but Will and Armstrong were put to work in the kitchen once again where they fulfilled their duties surrounded by clerics, some sporting large white aprons over their black garb. Will had not confided to Armstrong what he had discovered in the night, thinking that Father Jacques' personal life was his own affair and somehow he did not relish the bawdy remarks which would be forthcoming should Armstrong hear of the liaison.

At a break in their duties, they wandered out into the yard. Will was anxious to speak to Armstrong without being overheard. As they stood close together, hearing the muffled sounds of horses shifting in their stalls and the occasional exchange between those working in the stables, he expressed his concerns about moving around Paris and gathering information as to the whereabouts of Gaston.

'Aye,' said Armstrong. 'And time is not on our side. Let us hope that the good Father is making arrangements for us to leave soon. Then he grinned. 'I don't fancy being taken for a priest for much longer. It doesn't suit me.'

Will patted him on the shoulder. 'I think we can only pass as men of the cloth while we are with Father Jacques. No doubt he will have some ideas for disguise once we reach Paris. We shall have to trust his judgement.'

Armstrong did not look convinced.

After the midday meal had been served and cleared, Will retired to their chamber and began the arduous process of writing to Reeves to alert him of what progress they had made. Armstrong paced around the room as he was doing so, occasionally making less than helpful remarks.

'You've nothing to tell the man.'

'Surely it is dangerous. What if the letter falls into the wrong hands?'

'Are you certain of the code?'

At length, Will lost patience, the constant remarks interrupting his flow of thought. 'For the love of heaven, man, stop your prattling,' he hissed. 'And stop speaking so freely and loudly. Have you forgotten that you are supposed to have a speech impediment? Walls have ears. No doubt the good fathers are used to keeping secrets but it is unwise to drop your guard.'

'Sorry sir, I keep forgetting.'

'And *don't* call me sir.'

Will could sense Armstrong's restlessness. He stopped his writing for a moment.

'Why don't you take a walk in the grounds, Duncan? Clear your head and keep an eye out for any lurking spies.'

'What! You think there may be those spying on the good Father?'

'No, I don't. But it will do no harm to take a look around the place and take note of hiding places and ways of escape. You never know …'

Armstrong was delighted to be given a task and he paused only to shrug on his coat above his black cassock and make sure that his dagger was about his person, before he was striding out of the room and down the stairs to the main entrance.

With relief, Will settled down to finishing his letter.

***

Armstrong set himself the task of walking round the perimeter of the estate. He saw a few priests at work. Some were in a workshop mending a variety of implements and furniture and there was a blacksmith shoeing horses in a forge. Armstrong was tempted to go into the forge and stand by the fire but he didn't trust himself to play the dumb idiot and, although the language was beginning to come back to him, he knew that if he spoke in French he would betray himself as a foreigner. So he walked quickly on, his eyes darting everywhere, occasionally peering into barns and sheds but all was quiet and he could see no sign of movement.

He walked briskly, making a note of potential hiding places as he headed for the woods at the edge of the estate; there was no shortage of hiding places. Once, he peered into a deserted barn and, checking he was not observed, climbed up to a hayloft which afforded some excellent places of concealment behind the sweet-smelling hay stored there. He stifled a sneeze as he came down the ladder and smiled to himself as he remembered their brush with death when they'd journeyed from the coast to the farm, concealed in the haycart. He went out of the barn and continued his journey. He was enjoying his release from kitchen duties and the exercise and he determined to reach the wood before he turned back, but it was a fair distance. When finally he entered it, he explored one or two paths and some dense patches of undergrowth which could give cover to someone wishing to escape. The short January afternoon light hardly penetrated through the closely packed trees and there were great pools of darkness around him. He frowned, retraced his steps and had nearly reached the edge of the wood when something made him stop.

It wasn't even a sound; nothing he could identify, just an awareness, a feeling. He knew, instinctively, that there was a presence nearby and all his senses were immediately alert.

He stood still and listened, reaching for his dagger with his left hand. There was silence now, not the squeak of an animal or the sound of the wind in the trees nor even the tell-tale snap of a twig. But he was certain there had been movement.

Here amongst the trees it was so gloomy that it was difficult to make out any details. He did not move but the hairs rose on the back of his neck as he screwed up his eyes to stare around him.

There's someone here. Someone watching me; I swear it.

Very slowly, he took his dagger from its sheath and then, suddenly, something caught his eye; something metallic, something man made, and he knew exactly what it was. And it was very close.

Chapter Fourteen

He didn't hesitate then. In one swift movement he thrust his dagger forward and lunged at a shadowy figure. An armed figure. There was a shriek as his dagger found its target, not in the man's heart but in the top of his leg, enough to wound and stop him going anywhere at speed but not to kill. Armstrong pulled the dagger away and then leant forward, throwing his weight against his would-be assailant until the man staggered back, tripped over and landed on the ground. As he tried to crawl away, Armstrong put a foot on his chest, pinning him down. He leant towards him then, the adrenaline coursing through his body, and was about to shout out some curses when he remembered that he was supposed to be a dumb idiot and managed to control himself and content himself with a few choice grunts.

The man was writhing beneath him, clutching his leg, still moaning and shrieking, cursing in French. Armstrong said nothing but leant down and grabbed the short sword which lay beside the man, then, sweating and grunting, he dragged him along the ground, considerably hampered by the lack of an arm. Luckily his assailant was not heavy and, when Armstrong reached the edge of the trees where there was more light, he could see him more clearly. He was wearing peasant's dress and was young, his face twisted in pain and terror.

A young poacher, no doubt.

Armstrong hesitated. If he had trusted himself to speak, he would have challenged him and asked him what he was doing lurking in the woods. As it was, he put his dagger in his belt, kicked at him as he was crawling away and then made off with the young man's sword.

He ran in the direction of the house, looking back over his shoulder once or twice, but saw no one following him. As he passed the forge and the workshops, they were in darkness and it was clear that outside work had ceased for the day. By the time he reached the house, it was fully dark and, although he was greeted with civil nods and smiles as he stumbled through the main entrance, he didn't return them and ran straight to the chamber he shared with Will.

He burst in through the door and then stopped abruptly. Will was seated at a table and opposite him was Father Jacques. They were deep in conversation and sharing a bottle of wine.

Armstrong's appearance must have shocked Will for he stood up and came towards him.

'Pierre,' he said. And for a moment Armstrong stared at him until his thoughts calmed and he remembered his false identity.

'Has something happened?' continued Will. 'You look mighty disordered.'

Armstrong hesitated, looking first at Will and then at Father Jacques. Then he strode forwards and placed the short sword on the table beside the bottle of wine.

Father Jacques picked it up and examined it. He said nothing but looked questioningly at Armstrong.

'I took a walk, Father,' said Armstrong. I was in need of fresh air and exercise. And then in your woods I came across a young man …'

Will frowned, looking at the sword. 'Were you attacked?'

Armstrong shook his head. 'Didn't give him a chance.'

Father Jacques looked up sharply. 'Tell me you did not kill him?'

'No. I stabbed him in the leg and left him at the edge of the wood. He'll live, though his leg will be mighty sore.'

Father Jacques poured a glass of wine for Armstrong and then both he and Will questioned him closely about the appearance of the young man.

'It is not unusual for poachers to come into my woods,' he said.

Will picked up the sword and examined it. 'Yet this is not the weapon of a peasant,' he said quietly, looking across at Father Jacques. 'What are your thoughts, Father?'

'I hardly know what to think,' he said. 'At the very least it is an exceedingly worrying episode and it may mean …' He didn't finish the sentence and instead, got to his feet and began to pace up and down.

'Are you thinking that the man's garb is a disguise and that your activities here may be under suspicion, Father?'

He stopped pacing and sighed. 'It is possible, I suppose,' he said. 'Though, until now, I truly believe that operating as I do, in plain sight, continuing with the instruction of young men who feel they have a calling to the priesthood, no-one has reason to doubt my movements.'

He turned to Armstrong, frowning. 'In the heat of the moment, did you speak to the young man?'

Armstrong shook his head. 'No, sir. I was about to, but I remembered my disguise just in time. I grunted a lot.'

Will suppressed a smile and Father Jacques continued.

'Good. Then he will not have had cause to suspect you were not a native.' He paused. 'There may be an innocent explanation, of course. Perhaps he was a poacher who had stolen a sword – though that would hardly help him in pursuit of game. Perhaps he had simply lost his way.'

They discussed various reasons for the young man's presence in the woods and came to no obvious conclusion, but it was clear that Father Jacques was unsettled. Eventually, he left them, telling them to present themselves, as usual, to help in the kitchens to prepare the evening meal. At the door, he hesitated.

'Not all my plans are in place,' he said, looking at Armstrong, 'but in view of your experience, I think it is prudent if we leave for Paris tomorrow.'

'Have you any news of Gaston?' asked Will.

Father Jacques shook his head. 'None. But I have contacts in the capital. If there is any news of him, we shall hear it there.'

When he had left the room, Will and Armstrong exchanged looks. 'Do you think he knows Gaston is not a man?' asked Armstrong.

Will shrugged. 'He probably knows more than he is telling us.' He frowned. 'I'm proud of you, Duncan, fending off an attacker. Are you hurt?'

'He was only a young lad,' said Armstrong. 'If it had not been for the weapon he carried, I'd have agreed with the Father and dismissed him as a peasant looking to trap a rabbit or a bird for the pot, but …'

'But?'

'I don't know, sir. Something wasn't right. If he'd been poaching, then surely he would have run off, not attacked me. And if he had been lost, he would have sought my help.'

'Well, we shall be away from here tomorrow, if Father Jacques can arrange it.'

Duncan nodded, then changed the subject. 'Did you finish your letter?'

'The letter to Reeves? Yes, and Father Jacques has arranged for it to be taken to Pipette who will get it back over the water.'

'Then you will have said nothing in it about leaving for Paris tomorrow.'

'No, of course not. It was only after hearing of your experience that the plan was brought forward. Why do you ask?'

'In case it is intercepted. If that young swordsman is nearby and somehow gets his hands on it and if he is acting for our enemies …' Armstrong did not finish his sentence.

'Then he could report our departure to them,' finished Will. 'I catch your drift. Would you recognise him if you saw him again?'

'I don't know,' said Armstrong. 'Probably. Do you think he might be one of Father Jacques' servants?'

As they made their way down the stairs and were about to enter the kitchen, Will put his hand on Armstrong's shoulder. 'We must be extra vigilant, Duncan,' he whispered.

But although Armstrong examined every face he saw among the priests and servants, none fitted the form or features of the young man who had attacked him. After the evening meal and prayers, when Father Jacques once again summoned them to his presence, Armstrong was able to reassure him that, as far as he could tell, a spy was not lurking in the household.

'I am relieved to hear that,' said Father Jacques, 'But we shall set off for Paris tomorrow. I will accompany you and we shall leave as soon after dawn as possible. As I'm sure you know, it will be a long journey; Paris is some 200 miles distant.'

'Where will we stay on the way?' asked Armstrong.

Father Jacques stretched and yawned. 'At monasteries, at the houses of fellow priests. It is a journey I make reasonably often, though, I must confess, not often in the winter months, and my fellow men of God are well used to giving travellers food and rest.'

'And may I ask if these fellow priests and monks we shall visit are also of your persuasion, Father?' asked Will.

'Royalists, you mean?'

Will nodded.

Father Jacques did not answer for some time but sat in his chair, his fingers steepled together and regarded Will silently.

'I beg your pardon, Father,' said Will, at last. 'I was perhaps being indiscreet?'

Father Jacques smiled. 'No, not indiscreet exactly. But in these difficult times we have all learnt to keep our thoughts, and our loyalties, to ourselves. Even in a house of God there are those who overhear whispered conversations.'

Armstrong interrupted. 'Will we not be suspected?' he asked. 'If we are asked about our faith, where we come from, why we are travelling to Paris? This disguise is all very well but if we are closely questioned…'

Father Jacques spread his arms. 'My good friend, you have seen how my brothers behave here. They have been trained not to probe into the backgrounds of their fellow students but to concentrate on their domestic work and on their studies. If we are questioned when we are travelling, we shall say that Etienne and his friend Pierre are from my region, that Etienne is a student of mine who is seeking further instruction and has been offered a place in a Parisian community and that you, Pierre, are a priest who has been badly wounded in an accident and are seeking help from a medical man in the capital.' He stretched out his hand to Armstrong and patted his good arm. 'Just so long as you remember to act dumb when we are in company, all should be well.'

'It seems you have thought of everything,' said Will, getting to his feet. 'Thank you Father, for all you are doing for us. I'm sure you want to retire now as we have such an early start.'

'Indeed. I have a few more tasks, but you should both get some rest and I shall see you as soon as the sun rises.'

In their chamber, Will lay awake as Armstrong snored loudly in the truckle bed beside him. There was so much whirling around in his head that sleep would not come and he at length abandoned himself to his thoughts.

Father Jacques seems very confident that our disguise will work for us but we should be easily uncovered. Should we trust him? Although he has taken priestly vows, it seems he has no hesitation in breaking them. He obviously does not observe the rule of chastity and nor does he rate truthfulness highly. What an artful web of lies he has constructed to give us cover.

Then, from overhead, he heard, once more, some shuffling and creaking and the sound of a woman's giggle, quickly stifled and he thought once again of the encounter he had had with the beautiful young woman outside the stables.

She, too, is taking risks. Who is she? Do the other brothers here know of her relationship with Jacques?

At last he slept, but his dreams were full of the face – and the body – of that mysterious woman and he felt underslept and unsettled when he and Armstrong were roused by Father Jacques while it was still dark.

'There is a little food prepared for you in the kitchen,' he said. 'But please eat it with all haste. Dawn is not far off.'

He walked towards the door and then turned. As soon as you are ready we will meet at the stables.'

Will and Armstrong stumbled about, dressing and gathering their meagre goods together as fast as they were able before going down the stairs as quietly as they could, to take a bowl of chocolate and some freshly baked bread which was served to them by a yawning young priest. While they were eating, the sky began to lighten, so they ate quickly and then, shouldering their haversacks, they walked out of the back door of the kitchen onto the cobbled yard.

The light coach in which they had travelled to the house was waiting for them outside the stables, the two horses already harnessed, their heads being held by a stable boy.

Will and Armstrong climbed inside and before long, they were joined by Father Jacques. He had just given the driver instructions to move off when Armstrong suddenly drew in his breath sharply. He had been looking out of the window of the coach, back towards the stables.

'That's him!' he whispered to the others.

'Your assailant? Are you sure?' Father Jacques looked out but there was no one in sight.

'I cannot be certain. I only had a glimpse and he was moving in the trees behind the stables,' said Armstrong, 'But he had the same build – and he was dragging his left leg.'

'He was limping?

'Yes, he couldn't disguise his limp.'

Father Jacques frowned. 'I cannot believe that any of the servants know of my royalist sympathies.' He scratched his head and frowned. 'It is possible, I suppose, that an enemy agent has infiltrated my household though I find that hard to believe.'

But when the coach turned down the main drive and out of sight of the stables, he ordered the driver to stop, leapt down and ran back into the house. When he emerged, breathless, some minutes later, and ordered the driver to move on, he turned to the others.

'I have ordered someone to keep watch for the intruder,' he said quietly. 'We need to identify him.'

Will said nothing and just nodded but he had a good idea to whom he had given the instructions. It would have been to someone he trusted utterly and his mind went back to that stifled laughter he had heard in the night, and smiled.

The mystery woman.

Chapter Fifteen

As they travelled East, Will and Armstrong spoke more freely about the mission with which they had been charged. Father Jacques listened intently as they explained what had gone before, how Will had inadvertently caused his own brother to be murdered and how the high-profile double agent had been hiding in plain sight in the British Government and had caused so many royalist agents in France to be exposed and arrested.

'Ah, Vicomte de Menou,' said Father Jacques. 'As I told you, I know of him but we have never met. I can understand how your masters thought he was a royalist. He comes from an aristocratic family and it would be natural to think he would oppose Bonaparte. You say he was highly regarded and trusted by your people?'

'Yes,' said Will. 'When he was in England, de Menou went by the name of Barker. Reeves told us that Barker had fled from France at the time of the Revolution and been accepted into high society in London and, in due course, trusted to run royalist agents in France. Obviously, he was not what he seemed and was playing a long game.'

'So,' said Jacques. 'He is also, no doubt, in some part responsible for the closure of so many safe houses and places where royalists can find refuge?'

Will nodded. 'I have no doubt that this is true. Both Reeves and Pipette told us to be wary of making contact with any of these as things change from day to day. Those who have been operating under cover for months, or even years, have been exposed. She urged us to trust no one, particularly in Paris where Fouché and his men are so active. And particularly now, when Bonaparte has returned to the capital.

'Ah yes, Fouché will be on high alert. He will round up any he suspects of disloyalty to the regime, any who might make another attempt on Napoleon's life.'

'Is an attempt on his life likely?' asked Armstrong.

Jacques shrugged. 'I know of no plans to assassinate him but why would I? I act separately from the royalist agents. Few know of my activities in bringing royalists to and from the coast, only one or two trusted friends who pass on to me the names of those in trouble. And I always make enquiries before I agree to help; *and* I insist that those I help never reveal my name or where I live.'

'You are very discreet, Father.'

'Discretion comes with my job,' said Jacques. Then he lowered his voice, even though the driver was one of his staff. 'And, of course, I charge you, too, to keep my name and my activities a secret.'

'Certainly we shall,' said Will, and Armstrong cleared his throat. 'We are grateful to Pipette and our farmer friend for passing us on to you, Father,' he said.

'They are the only ones who know of my activities here,' said Jacques.

'But you have contacts in Paris and elsewhere?'

'Naturally, I have many contacts and because of my work I can travel freely between ecclesiastical houses. But very few of these contacts know about this secret life and those who do I would trust with my life.'

Will nodded and shifted in his seat.

And I wonder who else knows of his other secret life? He can hardly hide the fact from his household that he has a mistress, can he?

But then Will thought about the layout of Jacques' house. The chamber where he and Armstrong had slept was at the top of a turret, directly beneath the one occupied by the good Father. There were no other bedchambers near it. Perhaps it *was* possible that the beautiful stranger crept in secretly.

As they travelled they encountered few other vehicles on the road – an occasional cart, a few private coaches and they passed a large diligence being pulled by six horses, but few long journeys were undertaken at this time of year and for the first part of the journey they had the road largely to themselves.

They made good progress, the pair of horses moving at a steady trot on the rougher parts of the road and being urged into a canter when the road was smoother. They only stopped once during the day, at a small priestly establishment, to take refreshment and relieve themselves and for the horses to be changed. Will marvelled at how relaxed Father Jacques seemed when speaking to those who served them food and looked after the horses. It was clear that he made this journey regularly for it seemed he was known to everyone and he passed the time of day with them and asked after their families. Will and Armstrong said very little, keeping up the pretence of being sober and obedient men of God, though at one point, Armstrong tripped on a cobble and let out an oath. Father Jacques looked shocked and reprimanded him in front of the onlookers and Armstrong tried to look suitably chastened but muttered under his breath to Will 'at least I swore in French!'

Although they hardly relished the thought, they had impressed upon Jacques that they were anxious to get to the capital with all haste, so, since the weather continued dry, the decision was taken to travel through the night. They accordingly took on another driver and left their own to rest up.

Warmed by their meal, Will and Armstrong fell into an exhausted sleep inside the coach. Will woke once, confused and wondering, momentarily, where he was, until the jolting of the coach reminded him. It was still dark and neither Jacques nor Armstrong were moving, so he pulled the furs up to his chin and eventually dozed again.

When he came to, it was light and Father Jacques was shaking him.

'We have made excellent progress my friend,' he said. 'We are close to the town of L'Aigle and I know of a little roadside cabaret where we can break our fast.'

It was still early but the cabaret was already doing a brisk business and the workmen taking refreshment there doffed their caps to the three of them and Father Jacques obligingly gave his blessing to them all before ordering some bread and chocolate for Will, Armstrong and the driver.

Jacques clapped the driver on the back. 'You have done well, mon brave,' he said. 'We shall be in L'Aigle before long and then we shall change horses again and take on another driver.'

When they were back in the coach, Armstrong asked how far it was to Paris.

Jacques stretched and rubbed his eyes. 'We are halfway to Versailles,' he said and from there it is only a matter of a few miles until we reach the heart of Paris.'

'What has happened to the splendid palace at Versailles?' asked Will.

'Ah yes, that folly of beauty and extravagance,' he said. 'It was the focus of so much hatred during the Terror.'

He sighed. 'They say that it is largely abandoned and emptied of its contents now, though I believe there is some talk that Napoleon might use the subsidiary palace, the Grand Trianon as a summer residence.' He shifted in his seat . 'There are rumours…'

'Rumours?'

'It is well known that both Napoleon and his wife Josephine have had affairs and that their relationship is tumultuous,' he went on. 'It is rumoured that Napoleon is to separate from her and have their marriage dissolved.'

'And do you believe this to be true?'

Jacques rubbed his hands together. 'Who knows? Folk love to gossip. But if it is not it would be strange … after all, he and Josephine already have Malmaison.'

'What is Malmaison?'

'I have never been there but I have been told that it is the most beautiful chateau and estate and it is a place of tranquillity where Napoleon can work in peace.' Jacques pulled his furs tighter round his shoulders. 'It is only a few miles from Versailles, just West of Paris, so one cannot help but wonder if the rumours are true. If they parted and Josephine retained Malmaison then Napoleon would need another summer residence. Grand Trianon would serve well.'

'Why would he leave her? Any reports that filter back to England suggest that he adores her.'

'They say there is a deep affection, despite the infidelities, but he is desperate for an heir and it seems she cannot give him children.'

He frowned. 'And there are the assassination attempts.'

'At Malmaison?'

'Several. But all thwarted. Still, it must be unsettling. It is likely that Grand Trianon would be more secure.'

Their journey continued without incident. In L'Aigle they changed horses, this time at an auberge, and employed a new driver and ate a meal of soup and boiled meat with a few apples and walnuts for dessert but were soon on their way again. And so it went on, spending a night at another priestly house in the town of Dreux and then finally on to Versailles.

During their journey they had discussed what to do once they reached the capital and came to no solid conclusion but a way forward had to be decided and now that they were so near, the discussion became more pressing.

'We were given a list of safe houses in the capital by Reeves,' began Will.

'I hope you did not write any down?'

Will shook his head. 'No, we have committed them to memory; I have no record of them. But when we confided them to Pipette, she said that, to her certain knowledge, several of them had already been discovered.'

Jacques nodded. 'She would know, to be sure, but it takes time for news to reach her from Paris; her information may already be out of date.'

'What would you advise, Father?' asked Armstrong.

'To proceed with great caution.' He paused. 'You have passwords?'

Will nodded. 'It is to be hoped that they, too, are not out of date.'

Jacques scratched at his beard. 'You have already trusted me with the outline of your mission here, and please do not reveal anything to me which you feel might put it in jeopardy, but, assuming that you make contact with undetected royalist agents, what then?'

Will looked across at Armstrong who simply raised his eyebrows.

'In truth, Father, it is impossible to know,' said Will. 'Until we find out more, know where agents who have escaped are hiding, obtain more information on the likely whereabouts of Gaston, then we cannot take any useful action.'

95

'Is it your view that Gaston may be being kept captive?'

Will shrugged. 'Reeves seemed to think this was likely. Apparently this Gaston was in constant communication with his agents until recently but for several weeks has been silent.' He shifted his weight trying to relieve the ache in his buttocks. 'Pipette confirmed that this was highly unusual.'

'And this aristocrat, de Menou? Do you intend to confront him?'

Will laughed. 'No, that would, indeed, be foolhardy,' he said, not daring to meet Armstrong's eyes.

Not even to Father Jacques will I confide my intentions towards that double-crossing bastard.

'Then what is the point of trying to run him to earth.'

Will was beginning to form a reply when Armstrong answered for him. 'We need to find out how much he knows of the current royalist agents here so that we can begin to build a new network of those he does not yet suspect,' he said.

'Hmm. An exceptionally delicate task, I warrant.'

'Indeed,' said Will, looking down at his hands.

'And those royalists who are in hiding and seeking passage to England?'

Armstrong butted in. 'We have been ...'

Will shot him a warning glance. 'Reeves has arranged it, if we can get them to the coast, but ...'

'But, quite sensibly, you do not wish to confide any more in me,' said Jacques, smiling. 'That I completely understand. And nor would I wish to know more.'

The carriage rolled on and as they approached the city, the road became more crowded with vehicles and their progress considerably slowed. The afternoon was already drawing in and Will looked anxiously at the darkening sky.

'I shall be staying at a priests' guest house; I have business with an acquaintance of mine,' said Jacques.

'Another priest?' asked Will.

'Indeed.' He hesitated. 'He works in the great cathedral of Notre Dame, on the Ile de la Cité. I am to meet him there and then we shall be giving instruction to the newly ordained.'

'And may I ask if your friend knows of your activities for ... for the royalists?'

'No. He knows nothing of them,' said Jacques, shortly.

Will felt that he had offended Father Jacques and didn't probe him further. There was silence for a while and as they came closer to the central part of the city, he felt a sudden nostalgia for his time there with Jack, when they had been sent, as youngsters, to stay with a family known to their landlords, Clara's parents, to perfect their French language skills.

They had crossed the River Seine twice on their journey from Versailles as it looped and twisted its way through the city but it was difficult, in the semi-darkness, to make out familiar landmarks. However, he remembered quite clearly, the layout of the inner city – and how happy he and Jack had been studying there, exploring and living and working for a French family.

How lucky we were, looking back. Perhaps Clara's father knew, even then, that our families would intertwine, that Jack and I needed to open our eyes to life beyond rural Northumberland if we were to make anything of our lives. And my parents, too, must have trusted them, to let us go to further our education. But now I am disgraced and Jack is dead.

Armstrong interrupted his thoughts. 'Where are we going,' he asked.

Will addressed his reply to Father Jacques. 'Would it be too out of your way to drop us somewhere near the Bastille?' he asked. 'From there we can find our way to …'

Jacques held up his hand. 'No, do not tell me. As I said, the less I know of your whereabouts …' Then he gave a humourless laugh. 'The Bastille, eh? A significant landmark, is it not. The storming of the Bastille and the beginning of the revolution.'

'Indeed. And it is not far from there that we are going.'

'It is not much out of my way,' said Jacques. 'He leant out of the carriage and shouted out to the driver to let his companions down near the great bulk of the old prison.'

From then on they were silent, each alone with their own thoughts and when, at last, the horses were reined in, Jacques held out his hand, first to Will and then to Armstrong.

'Good luck,' he said quietly.

'I hope we shall see you again,' said Will, but Jacques shook his head. 'No, my friend, our paths, I hope, will not cross again, but I wish you success in your venture.'

'We are greatly in your debt,' said Will.

'Indeed,' said Armstrong. 'Thank you sir, for all your help.'

They could not see much, now, in the interior of the coach, but they sensed that Father Jacques was smiling. 'Go quickly,' he said. 'Two men of God going about their business should attract little attention. If you have to speak, Will, speak in low and reverent tones, and Sergeant Armstrong, remember to keep quiet and keep your eyes down.'

Before either man had time to react to the fact that Jacques knew not only that Armstrong was a military man but knew his rank too, Jacques laughed, opened the door of the coach and sprung out, letting the step down for them. Briefly, he clapped each of them on the shoulder, then jumped back into the coach, having instructed the driver to head for the Ile de la Cité.

'Good God, sir, he knew me for a Sergeant?'

Will did not answer but frowned as he watched the coach drive off, the pair of horses trotting off into the darkness, the lanterns front and back casting small pools of light into the gloom.

'Well sir, what now?'

'Now, Duncan, we head for the Café du Regent.'

Chapter Sixteen

Armstrong did not need to ask why they were heading for the Café du Regent. It was one of the addresses Reeves had furnished them with, a restaurant run by the mistress of a royalist spy.

As they set off at a brisk walk, he said, in a low voice, 'Do you think Pipette's information was true, that the establishment has not fallen under suspicion?'

Will shrugged. 'We cannot know if Fouché's men have it under surveillance but no doubt there will be plenty of activity there. People dining, a lot of comings and goings and, I believe, some cabinets for more intimate activities.'

'Cabinets? What are they?'

'Speak in French, Duncan!'

'Pierre.'

Will smiled into the darkness. 'A cabinet, *Pierre,* is a small private room where people can meet unobserved.'

'Romantic liaisons, you mean?'

'Mostly. But no doubt they are convenient, too, for other secret meetings.'

'Ah. I see.'

Will had memorised the location of the restaurant and he walked confidently forward, the way shown by oil lamps with a silvered reflector suspended on wires across the streets. There were still plenty of people abroad and occasionally he and Armstrong would be addressed as the crowd jostled them.

'My pardon, Father.'

'God go with you.'

Will acknowledged these remarks, mostly with a simple nod of the head or, occasionally, with a mumbled blessing of some sort. Armstrong kept silent and walked with his head bowed. When finally they reached their destination, they were both brought up short. The whole length of the wall of the restaurant facing the street resembled a great looking glass from top to bottom and the street lighting reflected back their own images to them, of two ill-kempt men in priestly robes.

'I was not expecting this!' whispered Armstrong.

'Neither was I! This is a grand establishment.'

'Is this a place where priests would dine?'

'We shall soon see,' said Will, pushing open the door to the inside where they were assailed by noise and laughter coming from a throng of assorted people seated at red marble topped tables. Waiters scurried about, serving food and wine, whisking away plates and wiping down tables. And around the edge of the room they saw some curtained off spaces which they assumed were the private cabinets. The place was elegantly fitted up. There were more mirrors between the piers and on the walls were sundry military decorations including paintings of spears, helmets and other martial emblems.

Their presence seemed to be greeted with no surprise and, indeed, they saw that there were already one or two priests in the restaurant. Noting them, Will and Armstrong exchanged glances, immediately moving well away from them lest their disguise be found out.

When they had been seated, with all politeness, they observed that the place was frequented by the military, too. Will, initially, was surprised at this but when he gave it further thought, he understood.

A perfect cover. Consorting with the enemy, no doubt this is a place where whispered conversations may be overheard when Napoleon's military men are in their cups. A clever ruse to make the place comfortable for soldiers.

A waiter was with them immediately, gesticulating and smiling and flourishing a menu before them which was so extensive that Will did not wish to show his ignorance about some of the dishes and ordered pâté, a platter of oysters some marinated fish and beefsteak for them both, refusing the waiter's urging to sample one of the many roast birds on offer, the veal and mutton, the various *entremets*, and the bewildering choice of desserts.

The man smiled and started to speak to Armstrong who had been keeping silent during this exchange, with his head bent. Will put a hand on the waiter's arm. 'My colleague Frere Pierre has been in a bad accident,' he said quietly. 'He had a terrible fall.'

Will gestured to Armstrong's empty sleeve. 'His brain was damaged and he lost an arm. He finds speech almost impossible, so forgive him if he does not reply.'

The waiter expressed sympathy and then dashed off.

'Better if we are not seen conversing with one another, I think,' said Will, and Armstrong nodded, though he did lean forward and whisper. 'Look to the far end of the room. I fancy that lady may be the patroness of the place.'

Will did not turn his head at once but let a little time elapse before he adjusted his chair so that he could look where Armstrong had indicated.

A striking woman was working her way amongst the tables at the other end of the room, pausing to speak to the diners, smiling, gesticulating, occasionally summoning a waiter to adjust a placement or take a further order. Will observed her carefully. He judged her to be over thirty, certainly, but still very attractive, wearing a fashionable high waisted dress of coloured silk with a low square neckline and long sleeves, over which was worn a short overdress of transparent muslin which created a shimmering effect. Her face, at this distance, seemed pleasing and unlined and she wore her dark hair in ringlets.

'She certainly seems to have some authority in the place,' he remarked, turning back. 'If she comes to our table I will slip some of our passwords into the conversation if I can do so naturally.'

All this time, Armstrong had been keeping an eye on the priests who were dining at the far end of the room. It seemed that they had finished their meal and before long he saw them rise from the table and make their farewells to other diners. He leaned forward to Will and jerked his head in their direction.

Will did not turn to look but gave a silent nod, preparing a story for the priests should they stop at their table. But the group just acknowledged Will and Armstrong with a smile and a bow and continued on to the great glass door which led to the street.

Will let out a breath and his shoulders relaxed.

Their food came with all speed and they devoured it with relish but although the patroness, if it was she, was still circulating in the room, she did not stop to speak to them, and it was only when the waiter had cleared their plates that she approached and asked if they had enjoyed their meal.

Will stood up and greeted her politely, saying that the food had been excellent and explaining Armstrong's silence, once again. She listened politely and smiled and it wasn't until she was making to move away that Will managed to insert one of the passwords into the conversation. She hesitated then, so slightly that an observer would not have found the hesitation unnatural, and then turned back.

'Sirs, since this is your first time in my establishment, I should like you to sample one of our special liqueurs, with my compliments.'

Is this a signal?

Will accepted her offer and sat down again, watching the woman walk away, continuing to stop and talk to diners before disappearing into the kitchens. He looked at Armstrong who simply raised his eyebrows.

When she returned, she had a waiter with her who was carrying a tray bearing a bottle and three glasses. He placed it on the table and brought a chair for her and once she was seated, poured out a measure of liqueur into each glass before going back to his duties.

As they drank, she explained to them where the liqueur had come from and expounded a little on the difficulties of obtaining some goods for her restaurant.

'Is this on account of the ports being blockaded, Madame,' asked Will, again inserting a password into his reply. 'I believe it is difficult to obtain coffee and other goods from faraway countries.'

She looked directly into his eyes then and this time she, too, inserted a password into her reply.

Will repeated it softly and waited while she continued to stare at him, possibly, he thought, sizing him up and considering whether she could trust him.

'Well,' she said, as she drained her glass. 'I am very glad that you have enjoyed your meal and the special liqueur. I hope I shall see you again, but now I must go about my duties.'

'Of course, Madame,' said Will, and both men rose as she got up. She offered her hand to Will to kiss, in the French custom, and as he bent over it, he felt a piece of paper being passed from her hand to his which he quickly transferred to the pocket of his black cloak. He said nothing but smiled and thanked her again, then called for the waiter to bring their bill.

It was not until they were a little way from the restaurant, standing under a street light, away from prying eyes, that Will was able to read the note and then it was with difficulty as the writing was small and faint.

'Ah, Sergeant,' he said. 'We were well advised.' Then in a low voice, he shared its contents.

'She has instructed us to wait until the restaurant is shut and the staff have left the premises and then come to the back door. It will be unlocked and she will be waiting for us inside.'

Armstrong drew his cloak closer. 'It could be a long wait.'

They stood across the street in a doorway, their priest's clothing making them almost invisible as they merged into the dark shadows. They watched as the restaurant gradually emptied, groups of diners spilling out into the dark cold night, some walking briskly away, some lingering to say their farewells, some climbing into carriages which had been waiting for them. The military men were the noisiest, joking and singing, staggering in the road.

'Officers back on leave from one of the campaigns, do you reckon, sir?' said Armstrong.

'Yes. Possibly they have accompanied Napoleon back from the Peninsular.'

Will watched the group of officers sharing jokes, slapping each other on the back, all, no doubt, drunk with the relief of having returned from battle in safety. He felt a stab of nostalgia as he remembered the camaraderie he had shared with his fellow officers – at least most of them. Armstrong's whisper broke into his thoughts.

'Take you back, sir?'

'That's all behind me, Duncan ... and for pity's sake stop calling me sir.'

Armstrong grinned into the darkness. 'Only do it to rile you, sir.'

Will said nothing and they both stayed huddled in their hiding place, but it was a good while before the last of the customers had left. The lights were on for some time after that, too, and then they saw waiters and other staff members scurrying away from the building, some chatting together, some too exhausted to speak. At last, the lights in the restaurant were extinguished and the place was in darkness.

'I reckon it's safe to go now,' said Armstrong.

They crept across the cobbled street, their feet and hands numb with cold, and went round to the back of the restaurant. Their eyes had adjusted to the dark so they could see the door quite clearly – and there was still the glow of candlelight which came from one of the rooms inside.

Will knocked softly on the door, then stood back, his hand resting on the hilt of his dagger, alert to any possible sign of danger, but it was obvious they were expected, for the door opened almost immediately. Then the restaurant owner ushered them inside in silence, closing the door quickly and silently behind them.

There were no niceties; no greeting or proffered hand to kiss. She put a finger to her lips and gestured for them to follow her, leading them down a dark passage and, at length, to a small door. 'Down there,' she whispered. 'You are expected.'

They waited for her to lead them but she shook her head. 'I will not be part of this meeting,' she said. 'Go quickly.'

And with that, she turned quickly and padded quietly back down the passage.

'Is this a trick?' whispered Armstrong, looking about them.

Will didn't answer but opened the small door. There were steep stone steps leading down to what he assumed were the cellars of the restaurant and he could see that there was a faint light at the bottom.

Chapter Seventeen

For a moment, Will hesitated.

'You go first, sir,' said Armstrong. 'I have my dagger and I'll watch your back.'

Will nodded and began to descend the steps, Armstrong close behind him.

When they reached the bottom and looked about them, there was no sign of life. There was a small table in the centre of the room and on it a candelabra in which were four candles already well burned down - the only source of light in the place. Round the sides of the room were shelves stacked with bottles of wine and most of the floor space was full of barrels.

They could see no one. Armstrong looked back up the stairs.

'I've heard no sound of a key turning in the lock,' he whispered. 'I don't think we are locked in so we should be able to get out if need be.'

Will simply nodded, then made his way over to the table, but there was nothing on its surface. He turned to Armstrong. 'All we can do is wait, Dun... Pierre.'

He had addressed him in French but Armstrong replied in English. 'Nothing else for it.'

Then, suddenly, there was a cough coming from the far end of the cellar. The men could not see it, but it was where a tunnel led into another large cavern and it was there that someone had been concealed.

Both men started and turned immediately towards the sound, their weapons readied, and watched as a man emerged from the shadows and then, as he came closer, he held out his hand. 'Gentlemen,' he said. 'Welcome.'

It took a moment for Will to recover his composure, then he took the man's proffered hand.

'Thank you, sir,' he said, reluctant to reveal anything to this stranger until he had assured himself that he was not an enemy, that this was not a trick.

'Louis Bayard,' he said. 'At your service.'

Will's shoulders untensed. The name was familiar to him – and to Armstrong – for it had been given to them by Reeves.

'I am delighted to meet you, Monsieur. I know your name.'

Bayard nodded. Then he brought three chairs from somewhere in the depths of the dark cellar and positioned them around the table. 'Come,' he said. 'Sit down and take a glass with me.'

Will and Armstrong sat down at the table and as Louis Bayard set about finding a bottle and some glasses, from where they knew not for they could see very little beyond the table, while they observed him. He moved swiftly and quietly, even though he was a tall and well-built man and when at length he sat down with them and poured them all a measure of wine, they could also see, in the soft light from the candles, that he was a good-looking fellow.

'We were told by your ...' Will was about to say "mistress" but thought better of it. 'Your friend,' he continued. 'That you, on occasion ...'

He did not know how to phrase the next comment, how to indicate that they assumed he was a royalist spy, but Louis helped them out by letting out a shout of laughter, making the other two look round them nervously. 'Ah, my beautiful mistress, Marguerite,' he said. 'She is the light of my life and a brave and clever woman. I adore her.'

'To Marguerite,' he said, raising his glass. 'And her continued loyalty to our cause.'

The other two raised their glasses. 'To Marguerite,' they repeated, and Will wondered whether there was also a Madame Bayard waiting at home for Louis.

Louis took a large gulp of his wine and then wiped his lips with the back of his hand. 'So, my friends, do you intend to keep this disguise?'

'We should be grateful for your advice on it, sir,' said Will.

'You came under the protection of Father Jacques, did you not?'

Armstrong frowned. 'I thought other agents did not know of him?'

Louis Bayard smiled. 'He likes to think that he operates apart from other groups, and, in truth, his cover is an excellent one for he travels for his work and is often accompanied by student priests, but he is known to us. Of course he is.'

'And he is not suspected by the Ministry of Police?'

'Not yet,' said Louis, frowning. 'But the net is closing.'

'So he is not known to Fouché?'

Louis poured himself another draught of wine and topped up the others' glasses. 'No, as far as I know, he is above suspicion by that weasel of a man.'

'And your group?'

'One of the few networks which has not been discovered, I am glad to say, but, with Napoleon recently returned to the Tuileries, Fouché's men are on high alert for any who oppose him. Or wish him ill.'

'Is that where he lives, at the Palace of the Tuileries?' asked Will.

'That is his residence in Paris, though he often goes to Malmaison, his residence outside the capital.' Then he paused. 'Though, with the Empress Josephine falling out of favour …' He shrugged.

'We heard there had been attempts on his life there,' said Armstrong.

Louis stared at him for a moment, then answered 'Yes' shortly before turning to Will. 'So, are you at liberty to tell me of your mission?'

Will looked across at Armstrong but said nothing.

'Come on man,' said Louis. 'Do not be coy. You know that I am trusted by Reeves. You would not be here at the restaurant if I were not.' And then, while Will was considering how to answer him, Louis continued. 'I suspect your presence here has something to do with the treachery of that man, Vicomte de Menou, has it not?'

Will nodded. 'We have been charged with finding him,' he said.

'Only finding him?'

Armstrong thumped the table so that the wine in the glasses slurped from side to side. 'If we find him, I'll not be responsible for my actions.'

Louis raised an eyebrow.

'He caused the murder of my brother,' said Will quietly.

Louis sat back in his chair. 'Ah, now I understand,' he said. 'You are the brother of Jack Fraser who unearthed the man's identity.'

Will nodded and Louis went on. 'Then, I can understand your desire for vengeance. Jack was an excellent agent. A man with a fine brain.'

'You met him?'

'Once, when he helped … well you do not need to know.' He leaned forward. 'I should have realised. You do closely resemble him.'

'Our other task is to try and discover the whereabouts of the agent Gaston and to assure ourselves that he is safe and well. Oh, and also to give safe passage to England to royalist spies in hiding; those whose identity is known to Fouché.'

Louis rubbed his chin. 'We are all anxious for Gaston's safety,' he said. 'He runs the whole network of royalist agents here and it seems that no one has heard from him in several weeks.'

Will met Louis Bayard's eyes. 'Do you know him, sir? Have you met him?'

Does he know that Gaston is a woman? Has this not been revealed even to other royalists here? Yet, if he knows, he would surely not tell us.

'No,' said Louis. 'He keeps his identity a secret so that even his own spies could not recognise him.'

'Then how do they receive instructions?'

Louis shrugged. 'Drop off points – and sometimes by word of mouth through an intermediary.'

'An intermediary? Then surely they must know his identity?'

Louis said nothing but turned to reach behind him and took something from the top of a barrel. 'Will you join me in smoking a cigar?' he asked.

Will shook his head and glanced over at Armstrong.

Is he remembering that time in Montagu's house when we detected that lingering smell of cigar smoke? When we were so cruelly deceived. God, I hope we can find that bastard De Menou.

Armstrong, too, refused the offer and they watched as Louis put the cigar to the candle flame and began to smoke it with obvious satisfaction and it wasn't long before the pleasing aroma swirled about them, bringing back for both Will and Armstrong that fateful moment when they had been duped, leading to Jack's discovery and murder.

Will felt the familiar stab of misery and guilt.

Strange how a smell can evoke such emotions.

Armstrong, however, was more alert to the matter in hand.

'Have you no idea, then, sir, where this Gaston may be hiding? Or, if he has been captured, who might be keeping him prisoner?'

Louis leant back and blew out a perfect ring of smoke. 'If Fouché has him, it will be a prize indeed, but there is no evidence of this. I have a colleague who has infiltrated Fouché's home and I suspect that that weasel of a man would have boasted to his wife, at least, that he had arrested a ringleader of the royalists.'

'Lord, sir,' said Armstrong. 'Your colleague must be a brave man!'

Louis nodded. 'He is working as a servant there. He tells me that despite Fouché's evident delight in arresting royalists and extracting information from them by torture, at home he enjoys simple domestic pleasures and is devoted to his wife and children.'

'Then how can he ...?'

'Ah, he's a man with many faces, my friend. He holds no convictions of his own but cultivates every political movement of the day. He was a maths teacher in Catholic schools who became a legislator. After preaching clemency for Louis the Sixteenth he then voted to send him to the guillotine. He became exceedingly rich but wrote a Communist manifesto, he served Robespierre then engineered his overthrow and his brutality against royalists has earned him the nickname 'Butcher'. And now he serves Napoleon – for as long as Napoleon rules. Though I suspect, if the Emperor should fall out of favour, the man's loyalties would switch once more.'

'A chameleon, then,' muttered Will.

'Exactly that. A self-serving and dangerous chameleon.'

Armstrong shifted in his chair and yawned. 'I'm a simple man, sir, and we have had a long journey. Tell us what we can do to help – and where we can sleep tonight.'

Louis smiled. 'Forgive me. You must both be exhausted. There is accommodation here where you can sleep tonight but please be

109

gone before the restaurant opens tomorrow. Our customers include many military men, as you saw, and your disguise is fragile. Anyone speaking to you will soon realise you are not priests.' He leant forward then, his elbows on the table, 'You say that arrangements have been made for a ship to transport escaping royalists over the channel. Can you disclose these arrangements to me?'

Will nodded, for, between them, they had memorised these before they left, and he and Armstrong explained how the escapees should travel from Paris and on to Beauvais, Amiens, Abbeville and finally to Le Trèport on the coast North of Dieppe, telling Louis the name and address of a safe house in Beauvais where they could lodge.

Louis repeated the name and address. 'A name unfamiliar to me, which is good, but was de Menou privy to it?'

'No,' said Will. 'Reeves has been doing his own private recruitment in recent months. This man is known only to him. He will keep your escapees overnight and then furnish them with a name and address in the next town, and so on. None would be known to de Menou.'

'And the ship? Where will she be and when will she arrive?'

Will's brain was becoming fuzzy. 'I can remember that the ship is called La Belle.'

'A French name? That is good.'

'No doubt the paint is hardly dry on the name she bears,' muttered Armstrong, remembering vividly their ill-fated voyage across the channel in the so-called 'Apus of London' when they were boarded by the Commander of a gunboat.

'I think Reeves said she's a galley,' Will went on, 'So she'll take a good few passengers and should make a speedy crossing.' Then he turned to Armstrong. 'Reeves will give orders that she will make the first crossing in February and aim to reach Le Trèport on the 14th of February or thereabouts. Is that right Dun... Pierre.'

Armstrong nodded.

'Huh, the feast of St Valentine, eh?' said Louis. 'And how will a British ship be allowed into the port, may I ask?'

'The Captain knows the French signals,' said Will. 'They were sold to the British by the signaller at Le Trèport. I believe he is an impoverished schoolmaster with a good many mouths to feed.'

'Then this galley will sail into port as a French ship?'

'Indeed. But she will want to be out on the next tide in case awkward questions are asked.'

Louis laughed. 'It seems that Reeves and his people have thought of everything. But what if my escapees cannot make it to the coast in time?'

'Then the ship will return again in a few days.'

Louis took another drag on his cigar and then he stood up. 'I am greatly relieved by all you have told me, gentlemen. I will pass this information on to those in hiding. But now you must go to your beds and in the morning rid yourselves of those priestly garments.

'But ...' began Armstrong.

Louis held up his hand. 'We shall find you something suitable to wear,' he said.

Will and Armstrong both rose to their feet, swaying somewhat from the wine and from sheer exhaustion.

'And tomorrow, we shall have to see if we can find any clue to Gaston's whereabouts,' said Will, stifling a yawn.

'And find out where that traitor de Menou lives,' said Armstrong.

'Your first task may be fraught with difficulty,' said Louis, as he picked up the candelabra and led the way towards the cellar stairs, 'But your second will be easy, for I know exactly where de Menou lives.'

Chapter Eighteen

Near Granville

Blanche de Valois stood at the window of Jacques' bedroom. From this vantage point, high up in the turret, she could see straight down the long, tree-lined drive which led to the gates of the chateau and she watched as Jacques' carriage, bearing him and his two newly arrived 'priests', bowled down the drive until it was out of sight. Then she turned away and sat on the edge of the bed, frowning. She was considerably unnerved by what Jacques had just told her when he had run up the winding stairs, crashed into the bedroom and spoken, between gasps for breath, of the young swordsman in the woods who had been sighted again and begged her to keep an eye out for him and if possible, to find out who he was.

Nothing like this has happened before. Does this mean that suspicion has fallen on Jacques? Why was the man lurking in the woods when he encountered that foolish Englishman? And has he seen them leave now? Has he been instructed to spy on Jacques? Will he suspect that he is headed for Paris and follow him? Or perhaps he is too badly wounded to do so.

She got dressed quickly, in the riding habit she had been wearing yesterday, and gathered up her things so that no trace of her remained in the room. She glanced at the rumpled bed and smiled at the memory of last night's passionate coupling, touching her lips and then putting a hand lightly on her breast as she relived it. She and Jacques were close neighbours and had known each other since childhood. They shared many secrets – but they each had secrets they kept from one another, too. Since her widowhood they had revived their friendship and it had soon flared into a mutual attraction. She knew he sometimes felt guilty and vowed to abstain but she also knew he was powerless to resist her and, in truth, the arrangement suited them both. As a rich widow, she had considerable freedom and she had no desire to lose that freedom by remarrying. And he, of course, could never marry.

But this development was worrying. She knew that he was a royalist supporter, as was she, and she had long suspected that he helped the passage of spies, but she never asked questions. It was better not to know and anyway, they had better ways of employing the brief snatched periods they spent together. Neither did he know everything about her activities. She smiled to herself then.

If he knew some of the things I have done, some of the risks I have taken, he would be horrified.

She took a candle and lit it before moving aside a tapestry beside the bed and opening a door behind it which led to a secret passage from the turret room to the outside of the chateau. As she crept down the stone stairs, holding the candle aloft, she wondered, as she often did, how many people had used this passage before her and what *their* secrets had been. At the bottom, she opened the small wooden door, hidden from view by a huge vine, looked right and left to make sure the coast was clear, closed the door quietly behind her and then headed for the stables. It was a perfect ruse. She was a skilled horsewoman and she often walked from her own house, through the woods, to exercise Jacques' horses, and the path she took through the woods came out just opposite the turret room. No one could guess that she had stayed the night.

She walked slowly round to the stables, mulling over in her mind how she might find out more about the mysterious swordsman. When she got there she greeted the groom and waited while he saddled up one of the horses for her.

'This mare's a mite skittish Madame,' he said. 'She's in dire need of a leg stretch. Are you happy to take her out?'

Blanche smiled. 'You know I always love a challenge,' she said, patting the mare's flank. She put her face near the horse's nose 'We'll have a good gallop won't we my lovely.'

The groom led the mare out to the mounting block and Blanche swung herself into the saddle and gathered the reins, then looked down at the man. 'I'm told there was an intruder in the woods yesterday,' she said. 'Have you had sight of him?'

The groom scratched his head. 'I ... well, no, Madame, I've seen nothing of an intruder.'

One of the stable lads was listening. He interrupted.

'When I was fetching hay from the loft earlier, I saw some blood on the floor.'

Blanche turned to him. 'So you think someone may have slept up there. Someone who had been wounded?'

The groom laughed. 'Take no notice of the boy. It would have been the cat with its kill.'

Blanche was still staring at the boy. 'Is that what you think?'

The boy blushed and looked at the ground. Blanche did not urge the mare forward but addressed the groom again. 'Tell me truly. Do you think there is someone spying on the Father and his household?'

The groom looked up at her, shocked. 'Spying Madame! Why should anyone be spying on us? No, if any fellow's lurking about it'll be some peasant looking to steal from us.'

Blanche was not convinced but she said no more. She did not mention the sword. Then she turned the conversation to the groom's family and the wellbeing of the lads who helped him before giving the mare the slightest squeeze to her flanks and setting off at a brisk trot.

'Have a care, Madame, she's a fiery one!'

Blanche simply raised her hand in response. The mare was, indeed, full of life and gave a series of joyful bucks which only made Blanche laugh. She was glad to be riding a beast of such spirit and she decided to give the mare a good gallop along the edge of the fields to tire her before she turned into the woods at the end of the property and crisscrossed the paths there, keeping her eyes skinned for any sign of the elusive man with a limp. However, there was nothing to arouse her suspicion; she met no one as she did a great circuit of the lower woods and then came back to the trees at either side of the main drive. She did not often ride here, for the trees were close together and there were no well defined tracks to follow but she could see that it would provide good cover for anyone wanting to observe the comings and goings from the chateau.

She had been out for nearly two hours and she had neglected orders that needed to be given and letters written at her own household – and also, her long absence might raise the groom's concern so, frustrated that she had been able to discover nothing of this mysterious visitor, she headed the mare back towards the stables. And it was then, just before she emerged onto the main drive that she saw something which made her pause.

It looked innocent enough. A small piece of white material caught on a bramble.

She reined in the mare and sat in the saddle looking down at it. She did not bother to dismount, for she knew what it was; a garter strap. A garter strap which had been ripped off a riding boot. She sat there, thinking, while the mare danced impatiently, eager to keep going.

No one comes into these woods except peasants who work for Jacques and they would hardly be dressed in long riding boots needing a garter strap to attach them to breeches. Whoever owned that garter strap was in a hurry, running from something – or someone – and too anxious to stop and retrieve it. If there is an intruder, he is certainly not a peasant. What is he doing here? What is he looking for? And what has he found out?

As she walked the mare back to the stables, she wondered, briefly, whether someone was spying on *her*. But then she dismissed the idea. She was a respectable widow who was often absent from her home and there only her maid, who she trusted with her life, knew anything of her secret life. And not just of her liaison with Jacques.

Even Jacques knows nothing of my other life. Or does he? He never questions my absences and tells me how they only serve to make him long for me more passionately. Yet, he has on occasion let slip a few hints at what he *does when he travels. Those two men who have just left with him for instance. They were no priests despite their robes.*

As she approached the stables, she saw the groom standing in the yard looking anxiously towards the far woods but then, hearing the sound of the mare's hooves, he swivelled round and saw her as she emerged from the avenue of trees beside the drive and trotted up to him.

'Lord, Madame, I was becoming mighty anxious. You've been out so long, I quite thought that fiery little mare had thrown you.

And what would Father Jacques have said if I'd let you ride her and you'd come to harm?'

Blanche laughed. 'I was only out so long because I was enjoying myself. She's a fine ride.'

'Let me help you down, Madame.'

Blanche hesitated. 'I wonder ...'

'Yes Madame?'

'It is market day in Granville and there is something there I need urgently. I had meant to instruct someone to fetch it for me before I left my house.'

'Shall I instruct one of the Father's servants to fetch it for you Madame?'

'No. That will not be necessary. I shall fetch it myself; it is because of my own foolishness, after all. Would you mind if I took the mare to Granville? It's a long ride and I think she'd be up to it, would she not?'

The groom started to demur but Blanche leant down and put her hand on his shoulder. 'I will take full responsibility,' she said. 'No blame will attach to you if the mare misbehaves.' She smiled. 'In any event, she won't. We understand each other.'

The man frowned and bit his lip. 'Are you sure, Madame?'

'Quite sure.' She leant down and patted the horse's neck.

And before he had time to raise further objections, she turned the horse's head and trotted smartly down the long driveway and out of the gates towards Granville.

The chateau was several miles from the town and Blanche put the horse into a steady canter along the track. Although it was still morning, she was only too aware how short the January day was and she must make her journey there and back before darkness fell. When she reached the town, she made for the marketplace although the mare was unused to so much hustle and noise and shied and pranced with her ears flattened. With some difficulty, Blanche dismounted and found a young lad to hold the horse.

Blanche knew that she stood out in the crowd as a woman of quality, wearing her finely made riding habit. She did not glance in the direction of Pipette's stall but walked slowly about the market making a few purchases and engaging in conversation with

116

others. She was well known and respected and she took her time, smiling and laughing, commenting on the coldness of the weather, warming her hands at a brazier where chestnuts were being roasted, before finally stopping at Pipette's stall and patiently waiting her turn to be served.

'Ah, good morning Madame,' said Pipette. 'How good it is to see you. I hope you are well?' They knew each other intimately, these two women and to an outside observer, their exchanges were entirely appropriate, one to the other, a fishwife being subservient to a well born woman of substance and waiting to serve her. Yet, the truth was very different. They knew each other's secrets and they relied one upon the other to keep them.

'Madame, I have your order ready,' said Pipette. 'Will you take it with you now? I'm surprised you came into town yourself, but then it is a fine crisp day. Did you bring your carriage?'

Blanche shook her head. 'I had a call to make and a desire to ride myself.'

'A fine day for a ride, indeed,' said Pipette. 'I will go and fetch your order. I have put it to one side behind the stall.'

Blanche followed her and as soon as they were out of sight Pipette came up close. 'This is a risk, to be sure. Is something amiss? We had no arrangement ...'

Quickly Blanche told her of the unwelcome visitor at Father Jacques' chateau.

'It may be nothing, of course,' she finished.

Pipette looked at her. 'A man in fine boots and carrying a sword lurking in the woods by the chateau. That is not nothing.'

She wiped her hands on a cloth. 'What has happened to those two men who came across the water a few days ago who I sent to Father Jacques?'

'They set off for Paris this morning, as did Jacques.'

'Then I suspect your wounded swordsman will follow them.'

'Do you know why the two men are here?'

'I do.'

'And you are not going to tell me?

Pipette shrugged. 'No need. But I will tell you this. Their mission is of great importance.'

Someone was calling to be served.

'I'm coming, sir. I shall be with you directly.'

Pipette shoved a parcel wrapped in muslin into Blanche's hands. 'Here is your order, Madame, all complete,' she said out loud.

Then she came in close to Blanche. 'I will alert those I can trust to see if this fellow can be intercepted.'

When the two women emerged from behind the stall, there was a cluster of people waiting to be served.

'Beg pardon, Messieurs, Mesdames,' said Pipette, 'the young lad who helps me is unwell today and I have no help. I am sorry to keep you waiting.'

'Madame Pipette is not to blame,' said Blanche, clutching her package and smiling graciously at the those gathered round the stall. 'It was my fault entirely, keeping her talking when she is so busy.'

As so often happened, Blanche's beauty and charm diffused any anger and everyone smiled and assured her that they had in no way been inconvenienced.

When Blanche returned to the lad holding her horse, she gave him a coin and he led the mare over to the mounting block in the centre of the market. Before she mounted, she carefully stowed her purchases inside the saddle bag, the package from Pipette last.

It was heavy and it did not smell of fish.

Chapter Nineteen

Paris

Both Will and Armstrong were so exhausted that they delayed any discussion of Louis Bayard's revelation that he knew the whereabouts of de Menou until the next day. They had been accommodated in a room above the restaurant and Marguerite had urged them to keep to their room until she should come to them in the morning. They had just risen and dressed when she arrived with a tray bearing bowls of hot chocolate and some freshly baked bread.

'I trust you slept well Messieurs?'

'I cannot thank you enough, Madame,' said Will, as she set the tray upon the table in the room. 'You have risked much for us.'

She smiled. 'Enjoy your breakfast but I beg you, keep to your room for now. Louis will come soon.' She paused at the door. 'And please make sure you leave here before we start to serve the déjeuner.'

Armstrong stretched and then settled himself down to enjoy the food. 'This is the best billet we've had,' he said, breaking off a chunk of bread and dunking it into the bowl of chocolate.

'No point getting too attached to it, Duncan. I imagine that we are to move on from here with all haste.'

'And in a different disguise, I warrant.'

Will nodded. 'We shall take Louis's advice on that. I get the impression that he is well used to dealing in disguises.'

While they were waiting they discussed their best way forward.

'We still have no clue as to Gaston's whereabouts,' said Will, 'so perhaps we should keep watch on the traitor de Menou first.'

'Do you think he knows the identity of Gaston?'

'It is hard to say. None of Gaston's agents seem to know her true identity. De Menou may have heard the name but I imagine that he will assume, like others, that Gaston is a man.'

'It is a brilliant ruse.'

'Aye,' said Will, rubbing his chin. 'She must be an extraordinarily brave woman.'

119

'It would give me great pleasure to run through that bastard de Menou and see him squirm at the end of a sword,' muttered Armstrong. Then a thought struck him. 'Will he know you, sir, if we meet him?'

Will shook his head. 'He is certain to have met Jack in the past – and he will know that he is dead. Even though I closely resemble Jack, I am hoping he will not make the connection.'

Their musings were interrupted by a knock on the door and Louis Bayard came in. He hardly paused to greet them good morning but came straight to the point. 'I have some disquieting news,' he said. 'I have come straight from meeting my agent who is a servant in Fouché's house and he tells me that Fouché and de Menou have been in regular contact during the last week. Obviously, he cannot know the reason for this but my man did overhear a conversation between Fouché and his wife.'

'And?' Asked Will.

'Fouché apparently said that he was near to unmasking the leader of the network of Paris royalists.'

'That is worrying,' said Will.

'Exceedingly. And even more worrying is that the name Gaston was mentioned.'

'Then we must act quickly,' said Will quietly.

'I have been turning this over in my mind all morning, my friends. I had a vague plan for you but it would have taken time – and time is what we do not have. If it is true that the noose is tightening, that both de Menou and Fouché are on Gaston's trail, you need to find out all they know and get to Gaston before they do.'

'Can we infiltrate de Menou's house in some way. Or Fouché's? What is your advice, Monsieur?'

Louis shook his head. 'Our agent in Fouché's house is well established and, in any case, Fouché keeps a simple establishment and there would be no possibility to add to his household.'

'And de Menou?'

'Ah, de Menou is a different matter. As you know, he only came back from England at the end of last year when your brother Jack unmasked him. Since then he has opened up his house in the 1st arrondissement and apparently all manner of trades people visit him.'

Will frowned. 'I thought builders did not work in the capital during the winter months.'

It is not normal, certainly, but it seems he has persuaded them to stay on. Apparently he is commissioning alterations of all kinds and new furniture and drapes in the latest fashion.'

'No doubt he has been amply rewarded for his work in identifying all those agents of ours,' muttered Armstrong.

Louis stroked his beard. 'Certainly he will have been rewarded. Financial and other plaudits will have come his way. Napoleon will have been pleased with him, as will Fouché. Though he hardly needs more financial rewards; he already has lands and a country chateau near Versailles as well as his house here in Paris.'

'So,' said Armstrong. 'Another couple of strangers going through his house will not stand out?'

Louis began to pace up and down, his hands behind his back.

'Pity we can't pretend to be soldiers,' said Armstrong to Will. 'We'd be good at that.'

Louis stopped pacing. 'What's that? Did you mention soldiers?'

Will glared at Armstrong.

'I just said we'd be good at impersonating them,' said Armstrong, not meeting Will's eyes.

Louis slapped his hand down on the table making the empty chocolate bowls slide almost to the edge. 'That is the answer!'

'Sir?'

Louis sat down at the table and leant back in the chair, his hands laced behind his neck. He smiled. 'I think that I am beginning to see a way forward.' He gestured to the others. 'Come, sit down and let me explain – and you must tell me if you think this is a solid plan.'

Will and Armstrong did as they were bid while Louis outlined his idea.

'Paris is full of returned soldiers,' he said, 'as, no doubt, is London. Many of them have no jobs and many are wounded. In the past I have helped …'

'I think I see where you are going with this Monsieur,' said Will. 'We could pass as returned soldiers easily enough and Pierre here,' he said, pointing at Armstrong. 'He has practice in remaining dumb. I explain to anyone who asks that the injury he sustained also affected his brain.'

'Yes, I was going to ask about this; his French is not good enough to pass as a native, whereas you …'

'So, how would this help us?' asked Armstrong.

Louis lowered his hands and drummed his fingers on the surface of the table. Armstrong eyed the bowls nervously.

'Folk are happy to give labouring employment to returned soldiers,' he said. 'I suppose they feel they are doing a service to their country in some way, though, in truth, the whole of France is tired of these endless wars.'

'So, would you be able to find some tradesman or other who is working for de Menou and could take us on to help?'

'I can certainly make enquiries. You are both sturdy and could shift timbers or bricks or bolts of cloth, I imagine.' Again, he glanced at Armstrong.

'You would be amazed at how adept Pierre is,' said Will quickly.

'So, if I could find some carpenter or other tradesman who needs a bit of help, would that give you scope to find out more?'

'And would that tradesman be a royalist'

Louis shook his head. 'It would be better not. What I need is a good fellow with skill and a family to feed who has little interest in politics and cannot afford to employ an apprentice.'

'So, we would not be paid?'

Louis frowned. 'I think, if I can find such a man, then I would ask that you had board and lodging with him.'

'Or, better still, that we could sleep in some outhouse at de Menou's place, perhaps?' said Armstrong.

'Possibly. But you go too far ahead, my friend. Let me see, first, if I can find such a fellow and if I can, if we can come to an arrangement.' He rose to go. 'Stay here for the moment and I shall return as soon as I can.'

'Marguerite asked us to leave before déjeuner is served,' said Will.

Louis smiled. 'Leave Marguerite to me and stay here,' he said. 'But for pity's sake keep quiet.'

Chapter Twenty

Near Granville

Blanche rode as fast as she dared away from the market in Granville towards Father Jacques' chateau. As soon as she was sure she was unobserved, she reined in the mare, walked her a little way off the road and opened the saddle bag. She drew out the package Pipette had given her. As she expected, there was gold inside – not fish - and also a coded letter which she read with great care, screwing up her eyes the better to see in the fading daylight. If the matter had not been so serious, she might have laughed, for the code used was set within a love letter which was extremely frank about the sender's admiration for her.

Why do the French consider that the English are not romantic? The passion expressed here is worthy of the most red-blooded Frenchman.

She sat still in the saddle for a few minutes, having decoded the text, and tried to work out what she should do next. The message within the letter frightened her – and she was a woman not easily frightened.

It all began to make sense now. For some weeks she had been on alert, her senses heightened. She'd not been able to shake off the feeling that she had been observed though she had told herself that this was nonsense. There were only a handful of people who knew what she was doing and all of these were trusted colleagues who she knew would never betray her. Why, even Jacques was unaware of her activities, less aware of hers than she of his. And then, suddenly, it dawned on her: her concern had all been for Jacques, afraid that he had become a target of suspicion, but it was not Jacques they had been watching.

The man in the woods. He and his masters, whoever they are, have no interest in Jacques. The man has been watching me. *Waiting to catch* me.

She shuddered.

What a fool I have been, coming to and fro between our houses

123

with such confidence. But if I am suspected, how has this happened? How can any of our enemies possibly know? And what *do they know?*

She sat there for a few more minutes, deep in thought, trying to make a plan. Then she became aware that the weak winter sun was already dipping towards the horizon and she turned the mare and galloped off down the track.

When she arrived back at Jacques' stables, the mare was in a lather, nerves aquiver. The groom came out to greet her and held the horse's head.

'I'm sorry,' said Blanche when she had dismounted. 'It was later than I realised and I did not want to ride in the dark. I'm afraid I pushed her too hard on our journey back from the market.'

'I'm glad she had the exercise, Madame. She needed it.' He started to lead the mare back into the stables but then stopped and turned to Blanche. 'You should not walk back through those woods alone, Madame. Give me a moment to settle the horse and I will come with you.'

Blanche was about to politely refuse but then she changed her mind. 'Thank you,' she said. 'I would be glad of an escort.'

The groom brought a lantern with him and they saw nothing untoward on their walk through the lower woods and back to Blanche's chateau which lay just the other side of them. She listened intently for any snapped twigs or rustling but the only sound was a squeal from a small animal falling prey to an owl. She started at the sound and then felt foolish.

The groom insisted on escorting her right to her front door and seeing her inside and she thanked him for his kindness, but as soon as the door had closed, she headed for the wide staircase that led to the upper floor, pulling off her riding gloves and hat as she went and calling for her maid who materialised at her side as if by magic, holding a lit candle.

When they had reached her bedroom, Blanche sat down, suddenly, on the edge of her bed and her maid held out a hand to her. 'Madame, you are trembling! What has happened?'

Blanche shook her head. 'Nothing Suzanne. I had such a long ride that I forgot to eat any lunch and I fear I feel a little faint.'

'I'll fetch you something from the kitchen at once, Madame,' said the girl, turning towards the door.

'And Suzanne, have the coachman ready the coach immediately.'

The girl stopped. 'You won't be going out again in the dark surely, Madame?'

Blanche nodded. 'As soon as I have eaten something.'

The girl knew better than to ask any questions. 'Shall I pack …?'

'Yes, you know what to pack.'

When the girl had gone, Blanche lay back on her bed. She was exhausted but she could not relax. If they were after her, if they had even the slightest suspicion of her activities for the royalists, she would have to be more careful than ever, for the stakes were higher than ever.

They won't expect me to travel by night.

Chapter Twenty-One

Paris

Will and Armstrong kept to their room but Will became increasingly anxious as the day wore on. They could hear below them preparations being made for the déjeuner, people moving tables and chairs, instructions being shouted in the kitchen and then the customers arriving and more buzz of conversation, laughter, comings and goings.

'It's making me hungry,' said Armstrong as he gazed gloomily out of the window and saw more customers making their way towards the restaurant along the street. 'Could we not just sneak down there and get some food?'

Will didn't bother to answer him.

It was not long after this that they heard footsteps on the stairs. When the footsteps stopped outside the door, they both tensed, looking across at each other as they watched the door handle turn, and when Louis entered, bearing a tray of food, they both had their hands on their daggers. Louis grinned. 'Friend, not foe,' he said, noting their stance.

He set down the tray. 'Help yourselves,' he said. 'It may be some time before you are served such good food again.' Then he was gone, saying he would be back shortly.

'Sir,' said Will to his retreating back. 'Have you …' But Louis simply put his finger to his lips and closed the door behind him.

Louis had not exaggerated. He had brought them a feast of soup, pâtes, beef and fruits which they ate with great enjoyment but Will fretted that the day was advancing yet no plan had been formulated. 'I hope our friend has had some success in his search for a tradesman,' he said. 'We cannot stay here, however pleasant it is. We need to make progress.'

When Louis eventually reappeared, his arms were full of garments which he lay on the bed. He was dressed smartly, wearing a coat with matching breeches and a waistcoat, and both men noted the small sword at his waist when he took off his coat.

Armstrong grinned, looking at the clothes on the bed. 'Working men's garb,' he said, picking up a grimy blue blouse and sniffing it, 'and well used, to judge by its smell! It seems you have had some success, then, sir?'

'The clothes are easy. I keep a ready supply of all kinds of disguises here.'

Louis grabbed a hunk of bread from the tray, broke off a piece and stuffed it in his mouth. He dusted the crumbs off his waistcoat. 'Finding a workman was not such an easy task,' he said, 'but at length I apprehended a carpenter outside de Menou's house. At first he was unwilling to entertain the offer of help but I could see how exhausted he was, heaving timber in and out of the place. And then I got into conversation with some of the other workers there and I told them I was helping returned soldiers and that all you needed was board and lodging and ... well, in short, they said they would welcome more help, that a midday meal was supplied by the household and that some workers were lodged in the outhouses there.'

'That is capital news,' said Will.

Louis held up his hand. 'There is one problem with the scheme,' he said.

Will and Armstrong looked at him.

'De Menou, it seems, will not have any person on his premises who he has not interviewed personally.'

'Ah,' said Will. 'No doubt he fears that royalists will be seeking their revenge. Do you think he will see through our disguise?'

Louis pulled at his beard. 'I think you need to be prepared to be closely questioned,' he said. 'As will I.'

'You? So he wishes to meet you, too?'

'I fear so.'

'Have you met him before?'

Louis looked down at his hands. 'We move in similar circles,' he said quietly, 'And I have a property not far from his, near Versailles. We have a nodding acquaintance but, of course, he has been living in England for years so we have not met for some time.'

'Could you convince him that you are doing charitable work for returned soldiers?'

'Yes, I think he would be convinced of that, but what of you? Can you pretend that you have been fighting for Napoleon?'

Will looked at Armstrong. 'Sergeant?'

Louis's head whipped up. 'Sergeant? Then you *are* military men?'

'Yes,' said Will. 'We both fought in the Peninsular. But we are not disclosing that to others.'

'It is a mighty risk,' said Louis. 'Would you remember the names of French regiments? Could you convince him you had fought for them?'

'My friend Pierre will act dumb and I will explain that he understands but cannot form words. I have a good knowledge of the French regiments we fought against. I think that knowledge will stand up.'

'And de Menou himself will have less knowledge than you,' said Louis. 'He is not a military man. But …'

Will anticipated the next question. 'I can adjust my speech,' he said, smiling. 'I can mumble and doff my cap and reply to questions in a rough accent.'

'Aye,' said Armstrong drily. 'He's a mighty good actor.'

'Well gentlemen,' said Louis. 'I checked and it appears that de Menou will be at his house all day. I suggest we go and pay him a visit.'

As Will and Armstrong changed with all haste out of their priests' robes and donned the workers' blouses, wide trousers and striped caps, Will looked over at Louis.

'This will surely be a mighty risk for you, sir?'

Louis shrugged. 'I take risks every day,' he said. 'If you can find out what de Menou and Fouché know about Gaston, you will be furthering our cause.' Then he smiled as he bundled up the priests' robes. 'And you have supplied me with another useful disguise.'

***

They travelled West along the Seine in Louis' coach to the 1st arrondissement and none of the men spoke much, each aware of the dangers of discovery. At last they drew up outside an elegant townhouse a little way back from the Place Vendome.

Armstrong peered out from the window of the coach. 'He does himself proud, this Menou fellow,' he whispered, taking in the elegant frontage and the separate entrance to the yard and garden.

Louis gestured to them to stay within the coach. 'I will go first,' he said. He smoothed down his topcoat, took his cane and hat and alighted, turning back briefly to the others. 'I imagine Menou will not refuse to see me, for I've heard it said that he is anxious to re-establish himself in Paris society.'

'Bonne chance,' said Will.

Louis nodded and then walked swiftly to the main door of the house and was soon admitted.

Armstrong started to speak but Will put his finger to his lips, and when Armstrong gave a questioning look, he whispered. 'You must act your part.' He pointed towards the top of the coach where the coachman sat, hunched over, the reins slack in his hands. 'I doubt the coachman knows his Master's business.'

Armstrong slumped back in his seat, scowling.

They sat in silence watching the comings and goings. Elegant couples strolling down the street, carts arriving to unload goods of all sorts into the yard beside the house and being greeted by the workmen there. There was plenty of noise, of hammering, of cursing, of laughter. And Will and Armstrong waited, banging their feet on the floor of the coach and wrapping the rug provided around themselves in an effort to keep warm.

The afternoon was well advanced by the time Louis finally emerged from the house and came to the coach.

'Is all well?' asked Will.

Louis nodded. 'Vicomte de Menou will see you in the yard,' he said. His voice was tight and Will could sense the strain he had been under. They got down stiffly from the coach and followed Louis under the archway and into the yard. They glanced round quickly and could see that work was ceasing for the day. Workmen were putting away their tools, some were bidding farewell to their comrades and heading home, others had made a fire in the courtyard and were huddled around it warming their hands. And yet others were going into the outhouses.

One of the men came over to greet them and Louis introduced

him as the carpenter who had offered to employ them. Louis had obviously apprised him of the situation as he only addressed Will while Armstrong stood by, looking down at the ground, secretly amused by Will's guttural accent as he answered the man's questions.

Then the back door of the main house opened and a finely dressed man came out and strode immediately over to Louis, putting an arm around his shoulders.

'So these are our two returned soldiers are they?' he said. Then he turned to Will and Armstrong. 'Which regiment and where did you serve?'

Will took off his cap and bowed his head, not looking at the man but answering politely in the rough accent he had used earlier.

'Hmm.' Then he gestured towards Armstrong. 'And your comrade? He does not speak?'

'He has difficulty forming words since he was wounded, sir, but he is strong and willing and can understand instructions.'

De Menou turned to the carpenter. 'And you say you can use more help.'

The carpenter nodded. 'The work will go faster with more hands, sir,' he said.

De Menou laughed, pointing at Armstrong's empty sleeve. 'Even if one hand is missing?'

'Missing because of his bravery in serving his country, sir,' said Will.

De Menou pushed Will in the chest. 'None of your cheek, soldier,' he said. 'I'll thank you to respect your betters.'

Will looked down at the ground, inwardly seething. The man may have been a supporter of Napoleon but he had all the trappings of an unfeeling, entitled aristocrat. He could well believe how convincing he had been in his role of spy in the British Government. And de Menou had caused the death of his brother Jack by blackmailing a vulnerable man. Will was suddenly overwhelmed by a fierce hatred for the man. A depth of hatred he had never felt before, even for his enemies on the battlefield.

De Menou turned back to Louis. 'Well, my friend, it seems your charity is doing a useful job in helping our returning soldiers. They seem genuine enough.' Then he addressed the carpenter. 'Dismiss them if they do not pull their weight,' he said. 'We want no malingerers here.' Then he shook Louis' hand and walked back towards the house. At the door he shouted over to Louis. 'Come and dine with me next week, Louis. It will be good to renew our acquaintance.'

'I'd be delighted,' said Louis. The sky was darkening and Will couldn't see his expression, but he could imagine it.

Chapter Twenty-Two

Granville and beyond

Blanche had snatched a light supper to sustain her and now she paced up and down her room trying to think of the best strategy to deal with the news she had received from England. She did not need to accompany the gold to where it was needed, she just had to get it to the next undiscovered agent and it would be conveyed up the chain until it reached those who needed it to effect the flight of the royalist refugees across the channel. Her instructions had come directly from Reeves and she knew they were true. The letter was written in his hand in the form of a love letter in his own particular style – a style which they both adopted and which amused them both. She had never met the man but she suspected that there was a passionate side to his nature. The message about the galley at Le Tréport was straightforward but the other news imparted was worrying.

Reeves told her that he had had no word from Gaston for weeks so he had sent new agents to try and discover her whereabouts and, if necessary, to help her out of France. Reeves enquired whether Blanche had any news – for she, of all people, would be the most likely person to have that news.

She had suspected that the handsome soldier and his friend were these new agents. Their faces would not be familiar to any of Fouché's spies. Were these the agents to whom Reeves referred? If only she had confided in Jacques – or he in her – but they were both too well trained, keeping their secrets close, even from one another. Could she have helped them? She knew Gaston better than anyone, after all. Had their enemies realised her connection? But then how could they? No one except her and Reeves knew that Gaston was a woman. Had he revealed her secret to others perhaps? Had she been unmasked?

She stopped her pacing and stood by her window, looking out at the dark. She closed her eyes and tried to think logically. No, if she was suspected at all, then it was more likely that it was for her other work. Pray God that she had not led to the unmasking of Gaston. If in some way she was guilty of that then the whole royalist network in Paris would collapse.

She came to a decision at last and called for her maid.

Suzanne came running. 'I have done all you asked, Madame,' she said. 'The packing is nearly finished and the coach is ready to leave at your convenience.'

'Thank you, Suzanne. Now, sit down, child.'

Suzanne looked up at her. 'Have I done something wrong Madame?'

Blanche sat down beside her. 'On the contrary, you have done everything right.' She looked at the young woman and then reached out and took her hand. 'I have known you all your life, Suzanne. Your mother was a loyal servant to our family and you have followed in her footsteps.'

Suzanne nodded and Blanche continued. 'You are the only person here who knows any of my secrets and I trust you above any, but now I am going to ask you to do something for me which will test your loyalty to the limit.'

The girl's eyes never left Blanche's face. 'Anything, Madame,' she whispered.

Blanche smiled. 'You have yet to hear what I ask of you.'

'I don't care what it is. I'll do it for you Madame.'

Blanche rose and went over to her armoire in the corner of the room. She returned with the package that Pipette had given her and handed it to Suzanne.

The girl's eyes widened as she felt its weight. 'What is this, Madame?'

'It is better you don't know, but it needs to be delivered with all haste and I cannot deliver it myself as I travel in the opposite direction.'

Then Blanche told her the location of the drop off place. 'Do you know where that is, Suzanne?'

'I know the village,' she said. 'It is on the way to where my mother lives.'

'That's what I thought. It is a full day's walk but I think you should reach it if you leave here at first light and walk as briskly as you can. I will leave instructions now for the cook to provide you with some victuals and some treats to give to your mother so that she knows I have given you leave to go.'

'Can I stay with my mother for the night? She would be mighty pleased to see me.'

'Of course. I shall be gone for some time. There's no need to hurry back here.'

'I shall wear my stoutest shoes and my warmest cloak and do exactly as you say, Madame. I promise I will not let you down.'

She stood up then. 'I'll finish the packing now Madame.'

Blanche looked up at her. 'You must swear to me, Suzanne, that you will never reveal this hiding place to anyone. Do you understand?'

'Never, Madame, I swear.'

'And if anyone asks, say that I have gone to Paris.'

Suzanne frowned. 'Can I give a reason Madame. The household may be alarmed that you have left with such haste and in darkness. Why usually you …'

Blanche nodded. 'I know. But I have my reasons.' She thought for a moment. 'You may say that I have had word that my mother is sick and I have left in all haste for Paris to visit her.'

'But you say you are not going in that direction, Madame?'

'No, I shall be travelling North. But it suits me that my household thinks I am going East.'

'East to Paris?'

'Yes. And this is what you must say, Suzanne, if you are asked.'

When Suzanne had left the room to finish the packing, Blanche hastily scribbled a note for the cook. She was about to put on her outdoor wear when she hesitated, took up her pen again and dipped it in the pot of ink on her bureau. She wrote a quick note to be delivered to the groom at Jacques' stables, thanking him for lending her the mare to ride and saying she was going to Paris so would not be visiting the stables again for some time. If he could not read, then someone would read it for him. It would do no harm for those at Jacques' residence to think she was heading to Paris. If the wounded swordsman was still there and had not gone in pursuit of Jacques and his companions, the news might somehow filter through to him, too.

Suzanne and another servant took the luggage down to the hall while Blanche went to the kitchen. A yawning scullery maid was still up and took the note, promising that she would convey the message to the cook immediately.

At the main door, Blanche kissed Suzanne on both cheeks. 'Be sure to give my warmest regards to your mother,' she said. Then she walked outside, followed by the servant carrying the luggage, and got inside the waiting coach.

'Where to, Madame,' asked the coachman. 'Your journey must be urgent to leave in darkness.'

'To Paris,' she said loudly. 'And there is, indeed, urgency. I fear that my mother is gravely sick.'

But when they reached the end of the drive leading up to her chateau, Blanche banged on the ceiling of the carriage. The coachman drew rein and bent down as Blanche opened the window.

'What is it Madame? Have you forgotten something?'

'No, my friend, I have forgotten nothing, but I wish you to turn left out of the gates, and not right.'

'Not going to Paris, Madame?'

'No.'

'Going to the usual place then, are we?'

'Yes.'

The coachman chuckled and they headed left out of the gates.

Blanche sank back against the leather upholstery and wrapped herself in the fur rugs provided. She knew she must try and sleep; she had a long journey ahead of her and a complicated task to complete but the jolting of the vehicle and the worry about what may have happened to Gaston, would not let her mind rest. Also, she was nervous that Suzanne would not be able to make the delivery.

Was I foolish to entrust her with such an important mission? What if she is apprehended on the road and robbed? I have put her in danger, poor child. Yet, if I had waited longer, I should not have reached Le Tréport in time to set things up there. From what Reeves said, there may be a good many royalists coming to the

135

coast fleeing the clutches of Fouché and his men and it is my responsibility to smooth their passage.

She shivered. Despite the furs, it was bitterly cold inside the coach and she gave a thought to the coachman who had no protection against the elements. Yet he had made no complaint at being asked to drive through the night. She smiled then. He was a good friend and had been with the family for years. She had not taken him into her confidence in the way she had Suzanne, but she had let him believe that her assignations further up the coast were of a romantic nature and he had entered into the deception with enthusiasm. He was convinced that she visited a lover on these journeys North and although she had never admitted this, she had often said to him how she valued his discretion and had sworn him to secrecy.

She could not be certain, though, that he had not gossiped to others while in his cups but idle gossip could do little harm and gave good cover for the real purpose of these trips.

Little did he know that she had a lover much closer to home.

Chapter Twenty-Three

Paris

One of the outhouses in de Menou's yard had been cleared to give accommodation to the workers whose homes were not close by. Will and Armstrong were shown to a place where they could sleep and supplied with a couple of rough pallets. It had served as a tack room before and there was still an all-pervading smell of saddle soap and oil used for cleaning leather which mingled with the more powerful stink of men's sweat. But there was a fire burning in the grate and a simple meal of stew was provided from the kitchen so the billet was not too uncomfortable.

Will made it his business to get into conversation with the other workers sleeping there. He and Armstrong had concocted a back story about where they came from in France and what had befallen them while fighting in Portugal. However, they soon discovered that their companions were simple men with little interest in ex-soldiers. Exhausted after a full day's manual labour, all they wanted was to fill their bellies, quaff some wine and get some sleep before the next day's relentless toil.

Before they settled down for the night, the men trailed out into the yard to use the privy at the back of the stables. As the newcomers, Will and Armstrong hung back and waited until the others had done their business before taking their turn. It was a deliberate ruse, meaning that they would have a chance to speak openly without being overheard.

There was a lantern hanging outside the privy and inside just a hole in the ground with planks either side, surrounded by a rough wooden fence. Armstrong gagged as he went inside, the stink of urine and faeces making his eyes water, and when he emerged, he whispered. 'Hold your nose, sir!'

When they had both relieved themselves, they lingered outside for a few moments, whispering together.

'We need to get friendly with the kitchen staff, Duncan,' said Will. 'They will know their Master's movements and they'll know who is living in the house with him and who comes to visit.'

137

'That's all good and fine, sir, and I'd be happy to cosy up to some pretty kitchen wench, but you have given me the role of a dumb idiot, remember!'

Will frowned. 'Aye. That might be a problem, but it could work in our favour, too.'

'How so?'

'People do not guard their speech in front of a dumb idiot!'

'Huh. The role don't suit me.'

'Can you think of another?'

Armstrong shook his head.

'Then make it your business to eavesdrop. Keep your eyes open and your ears flapping.'

'And what will you do?'

Will smiled. 'I shall do exactly as I am bid by our carpenter friend. I shall be a model worker. But we need to get inside that house tomorrow. Let's hope I'm not kept just sawing wood for him out here in the yard all day.'

'We'll have to take our chances then. I'd be no good sawing but I can offer my services as a strong hauler, if nothing else. And you can do the flirting.'

'I am out of practice at flirting, my friend.'

'Don't give me that, sir. You're a handsome ex-soldier. No kitchen wench will be able to resist you.'

'I am touched by your faith in me as a lover, Duncan!'

They started to make their way back to their billet when Armstrong stopped. 'What's our strategy with de Menou? Are you to murder him at once?'

'I'd dearly love to run that bastard through but I doubt I'll get a chance dressed as a workman; there's nowhere to conceal a weapon and besides, we need to garner information from him. By all accounts he's close to Fouché and the two exchange confidences.'

'So, it's a waiting game?'

'I fear so. Though I'm mighty impatient to move this business forward.'

***

But during the next few days, there was little chance to make progress with their scheme. The carpenter, though a fair boss, was a man of few words, explaining exactly what he wanted from them and overseeing them with a depressing vigilance. When Armstrong vented his irritation to Will, Will bade him to be patient.

'If we show willing and do as we are bid, he'll stop watching us so keenly,' he said. 'We must be patient.'

However, Will, too, was getting increasingly concerned at the delay. Though he was confident that those exposed agents would now be moving to the coast, he was worried that in playing this role, there would be little chance to communicate their situation to Reeves. Louis Bayard had told them that he would come to visit de Menou again to check that he and Duncan were conscientious workers, and they were relying on him to act as their conduit, but there had, as yet, been no sign of him. He voiced these concerns to Armstrong in one of their whispered conversations.

'What about our priest friend?'

'Aye. I had thought of that, even though he's not of the network, he may have gleaned more information.'

Armstrong scratched his head with his good arm. 'We'll be given Sunday off, will we not, sir?'

'What are you suggesting, Duncan?'

Armstrong grinned. 'Don't all good Catholics go to mass on Sundays?'

Will punched him lightly on his good arm. 'Indeed they do, Duncan. The good Father mentioned that he was staying at a priestly guesthouse near Notre Dame, did he not. And as peasants from outside the capital, we might well be curious to visit that great cathedral of Paris.'

'Important that we cleanse our souls, sir.'

'Indeed.'

Armstrong sighed. 'It's Wednesday today. A long wait until Sunday.'

'Still,' said Will. 'I may yet hear something from the kitchen.'

In an effort to inveigle himself into the household, Will had been taking empty platters and flagons back to the house before they were collected by the kitchen staff. He'd been thanked politely and though the cook and other servants there had been mildly surprised at this courtesy, they were grateful for it so he had begun to do it regularly.

On Thursday morning, as he entered the kitchen, there was such a flurry and rushing hither and thither that he picked up an unusual sense of panic in the room. As he put down his load on the table, he smiled at a young kitchen maid who he had exchanged pleasantries with before and asked her what was happening.

As she gathered up the empties to wash, she raised her eyebrows. 'Lord, it would happen today, wouldn't it?'

'What?'

She shoved him out of her way and another maid answered. 'The Master's only having a fancy dinner this evening and half the kitchen's down with the flux.'

Will thought quickly. 'If you are short, I could help serve,' he said. 'I served at table in the army.'

The girl simply shrugged. 'The Master's that fussy. He wouldn't like someone not trained.'

'I was trained,' said Will.

Somehow, in all the noise and clatter, the word 'trained' had filtered through to the cook. She was red in the face, stirring pots, giving instructions and thoroughly flustered but she turned then to stare at him.

'If you're Army trained, you might do,' she said. 'Go and talk to the butler.' And she pointed to a man who had just entered the kitchen.

Will went over to him. He had the air of a dignified fellow but even he was looking distraught. Will repeated his offer and gave his name as Etienne.

'What's your employment here Etienne?'

When Will told him, the man frowned. 'You're a carpenter?'

'No sir, I'm a returned soldier doing unskilled work. I am glad to get any job I am offered. But I did serve at table in the army.'

This was a blatant lie and Will hoped to God he would not be caught out.

The butler looked Will up and down, frowning and then, at length, he sighed. 'Come back when you have downed tools and I'll find a uniform and explain your duties.'

140

'Yes sir.'

'Thank you for your offer, Etienne. See that you don't let me down.'

'I won't sir.'

When Will told Armstrong of the arrangement, he was delighted. 'That's capital, sir. Perhaps I could offer my services, too. The kitchen staff could put me to work in some capacity, could they not?'

'Come with me when I report to the butler, Duncan. I'll see if I can persuade them to use you. But we must not appear too keen.'

'If they're that short, my guess is that they'll take the offer of any help.'

'Well,' said Will. 'It seems we have been aided by an attack of the flux. We must pray that we avoid it ourselves.'

As before, this whispered conversation was taking place outside the privy. Armstrong chuckled. 'We've visited the privy that often, our fellow workers may suspect we are suffering already.'

A little later, Will reported to the butler and suggested that Armstrong could also be put to work to help them.

'He don't speak, sir but he understands everything and he's strong and willing,' he said in his strong Southern accent.

The butler hardly glanced at Armstrong. 'For God's sake, man, he only has the one arm!'

Will didn't argue and Armstrong headed for the door when the cook yelled over at him.

'I don't care if you've only the one arm, son. If you can pile up dishes and scrub pans, I'll take your help.'

Armstrong turned back, glancing briefly at Will before heading over to the great china sink piled high with dirty pots and pans.

Will said nothing as the butler led him to a chamber where a server's uniform was laid out for him.

'Change quickly,' said the man. 'And clean yourself up.' He pointed to a basin of water and a jug which stood on a table beneath the window. 'There's water and a towel there and a comb.' Then he stood, tapping his foot on the floor, as he watched Will transform himself into a servant of the household. Then he led him into the dining room and explained his duties. There were two kitchen maids laying up the table and the butler shouted at them for their clumsiness. One of them was near to tears and Will said quickly. 'I can do this, sir. Why not send the maids back to the kitchen where they are more needed?'

The butler frowned and said nothing but after he had watched Will set the table with speed and an obvious knowledge of what went where, he shooed the girls back to their kitchen duties. Then he seemed to relax a little as he explained which courses were being presented and how to serve them.

'Is this familiar to you, Etienne?'

'It is not too different from regimental dinners, sir,' said Will, remembering some of the boring dinners he had been forced to sit through in his other life but grateful, now, for the experience. He had counted the places set, noting that the dinner was for ten people. 'May I ask who is coming to dine, sir?'

The butler sighed. 'The Vicomte is anxious that this evening is a success,' he said, 'but with all the refurbishment going on and so many staff fallen sick, everything is awry and I fear it will not be the elegant occasion he wishes.' He turned to Will. 'It is the first time he has invited guests of such importance since he returned from abroad.'

'May I ask who the guests are?'

The butler recited names unfamiliar to Will, except one, and when he heard it, it took all his self control not to exclaim with horror.

'So, sir, the Chief of Police is to dine here. That is an honour indeed.'

'Yes,' he said slowly. 'Joseph Fouché is certainly a man of influence.' He paused. 'I've heard it said that the Emperor is to ennoble him this year. The Vicomte was saying he's to be given the title of Duke of Otranto.'

Will could not tell, from the butler's tone, whether this was said with approval or not, so he simply nodded and changed the subject. 'When do the guests arrive, sir?'

'Almost immediately. We shall serve them wine in the main salon before they dine and when they move into the dining room, the kitchen staff will bring each course through and we shall serve them from the platters.'

Once the guests had arrived, Will helped the butler to serve drinks in the salon and took the opportunity to observe them all closely. When he handed a glass to de Menou he had to force down his desire to smash it in his face. Aside from being the cause of his brother's death, the man had an air of entitlement which made Will's gorge rise. De Menou took the glass and looked up briefly and frowned, addressing the butler as he did so. 'Who is your new recruit, Moreau, you did not tell me about him.'

'Beg pardon, sir,' said the butler, lowering his voice to a whisper. 'There is much sickness in the household. The man is working for the carpenter. He is a returned soldier and has some experience serving at table.'

'Ah yes, I recognise him now. One of Louis Bayard's charity cases.' As Will began to move away, de Menou turned to his companion. 'Louis Bayard is a splendid fellow. He has a country house near mine near Versailles. Doing good work finding employment for returned soldiers. I invited him to dine this evening but he had some pressing business. A pity. He is good company.'

'No doubt it was *extremely* pressing,' thought Will suppressing a smile as he refilled the glass of a fine looking dark-haired young woman who had been listening intently to the exchange about Louis Bayard. She was dressed in the latest fashion and her eyes were intelligent and watchful. She thanked Will politely and then asked in which regiment he had served and listened attentively when he replied.

Will continued his rounds but he couldn't get her face out of his mind. There was something about her which seemed vaguely familiar though he was sure they had not met before.

Joseph Fouché was the last to arrive and was greeted enthusiastically by de Menou though Will sensed some unease among the rest of the company.

He's turned on others. For now he is their friend but if it suits his purpose, he will turn again.

The butler went to serve Fouché and Will was relieved he did not need to go near the man. He'd heard him described as a weasel with a club foot and, indeed, he had the mean look of a rodent about him as he limped across the room to take his seat. Will shuddered and turned his back on him, remembering the accounts he had heard of the man's brutality.

Ye gods, what would he do to me if he had one whiff of my intentions?

Once the party had moved into the dining room, Will was fully occupied and had no time to think of anything but his duties as a waiter. De Menou had certainly provided a feast for his guests and it was no wonder that the poor cook and her staff were in such a dither. Someone had lit the candles and put a pretty decoration on the table and as the courses came in from the kitchen, they were placed in the centre of the table and it was Will's job to serve the company from the central platters. The etiquette dictated that any diner could ask for any dish to be passed to them to sample and this kept both Will and the butler extremely busy.

Soups were served first, then there were plates of roasted or stewed meats, poultry and fish. These were followed by dishes of hares and pigeons and finally there were petit-choux and a tarte de crème. And at the same time, the guests' glasses must be kept filled.

When at last the carriages had come and the guests departed, Will was exhausted, not only from the work itself, but by the strain of eavesdropping on conversations. He had kept a discreet eye on the dark haired young woman, too, and noticed that de Menou paid her a deal of attention, his eyes constantly watching her. And he came close to her on every possible occasion, putting her fingers to his lips and bending forward to whisper in her ear. She was nothing but charming in response but Will noticed the odd flicker of irritation pass over her face, smothered as soon as it occurred. He also noticed that she did not leave with the other guests but, after bidding them farewell, turned and ran up the stairs to the upper chambers.

The kitchen staff had almost finished clearing away when the butler asked Will to share a glass with him. They went into his chamber and the butler sat down rubbing his knee.

'A long evening plays the devil with my bad leg,' he said, then leaned back in his chair, stretched his legs out, wiped his brow and took a large gulp of his wine. 'Well, you certainly proved your worth, Etienne. The evening would not have gone so well without your help.'

For a while they exchanged pleasantries, discussed the evening and drank their wine but at length, Will yawned and rubbed his aching neck. 'I'm glad I could be of help, sir, but now I must get some rest or I shall be no use at sawing planks of wood tomorrow.'

'Of course. I must let you go. You've had a long day.'

As Will rose to leave, the butler got up, too. 'You could be a useful addition to the household, Etienne. Would you like me to speak to the Vicomte?'

Will hesitated. 'I would like that very much, sir, but for the moment I am bound to the carpenter. He has been good to me. But I am happy to help here if needed, after my working day has ended.'

It was very late when Will and Armstrong met up outside the privy. The other workers had retired long since.

'I need my bed,' growled Armstrong. 'Pot-washing's a tedious hard business when you've only got one hand.'

Will nodded into the darkness. 'You did well, Duncan. Did you pick up any useful gossip?'

'Aye, a fair bit.'

'And?'

Armstrong scratched his head. 'There was a lot of talk about the Fouché fellow. They were all wondering why he had come to the house. It seems most of Paris fears him. Then there was some gossip about the Vicomte and one of the guests.'

Will was suddenly alert. 'Which one?'

'Mademoiselle La Fargue.'

'The dark-haired beauty?'

Armstrong shrugged. 'How do I know? I never clapped eyes on any of them, did I? Had my head in the sink the whole evening.'

'What did they say about her?'

Armstrong yawned. 'They say de Menou lusts after her.'

'Aye. I could see that.'

'The servants say he's proposed marriage to her but she's taking

145

her time making up her mind. Apparently she's been staying here for the last month while her own apartments are refurbished and he never leaves her side. Dances attendance on her all the time.'

Will frowned. 'There is no doubt that *he* is smitten, but I'm not so sure about her.'

Armstrong laughed. 'She's a lady of impeccable virtue, they say.'

'Any other gossip?' asked Will.

'Nothing useful. Mostly rude jokes about other members of the staff – oh, and a lot of interest in the handsome new waiter.'

'You're making that up!'

'I am not. One of the kitchen maids is more than a little interested. I reckon she'd give you a kiss and a cuddle as soon as look at you.'

Will smiled. 'No time for that Duncan. Come on, let's get to our billet.'

But as they walked back to the outhouse, his mind was racing. Something was clicking into place. Something about the lovely Mademoiselle La Fargue. He needed to see her again.

Chapter Twenty-Four

By chance, an opportunity arose the next evening. Will enquired of the butler whether any help was needed and this was gratefully accepted.

'This damned sickness is raging through the house,' he said. 'Any help would be appreciated.' He put a hand on Will's shoulder. 'And I have not forgotten my promise, Etienne. I will find a time to approach the Master and suggest that he employs you. You would be a great asset.'

Will had no desire for another interview with de Menou. Although there was no reason for the man to make the connection, Will's resemblance to Jack might trigger some suspicion.

'I thank you for your kindness, sir, but I must continue to work for the carpenter for now. I would not let him down. Meanwhile, I can do a little work here in the evenings until the others have recovered. Would you have me serve at dinner again?'

'No need for that. The Master is dining out and Mademoiselle La Fargue is taking a light supper in her room.'

That evening, Will made sure that he completed any tasks he was set with scrupulous efficiency, from sweeping floors to polishing silver, all the time keeping his eyes lowered and trying not to notice the blushes and whispers of the kitchen maids who made every excuse to engage him in conversation. At last the cook clipped one of them round the ear and told them to stop bothering the poor soldier and to get on with her work. Then she called Will over, pointing to a tray covered with a muslin cloth.

'Take this up to Mademoiselle La Fargue, Etienne, if you please. The room on the top floor at the left of the staircase. She will be expecting it.'

Will wiped his hands on a dish rag and took the tray. He could hardly believe his luck. All the time he had been employed in other tasks, he had been trying to think of a way of making contact with her and now an opportunity had fallen into his lap! He left the kitchen with all haste in case the butler should see him and decide to take the tray up himself.

As Will climbed the stairs to the top floor he took note of the new hangings and plasterwork. Clearly the upper chambers had been the first to be refurbished and no expense had been spared.

De Menou has been richly rewarded for his spying work, the bastard.

When he reached the top of the stairs he turned left as instructed and knocked at the door in front of him, his heart hammering. He would have to be very careful in what he said and he would only have a matter of minutes in which to say it, otherwise his absence would be noted.

'Come!'

He turned the door handle and walked in.

She was sitting in front of the fire, reading a book. As he entered, she put the book down on the table in front of her and smiled at him.

'Ah, the returned soldier,' she said. 'Thank you for helping out. I fear the household is much affected by illness.'

'My pleasure, Mademoiselle.'

Will put the tray down in front of her and then straightened up. She was clearly expecting him to leave at once but he stayed there watching her intently. At length she looked up and met his eyes.

'It was a pity that Louis Bayard could not dine with you last evening,' he said.

There was a beat of silence. She registered no shock at his remark but without lowering her eyes, she reached for the glass of wine by her side and took a sip. 'You are acquainted with Monsieur Bayard?'

'Indeed,' said Will. He still did not move away.

'May I ask how?'

'He has given us shelter.'

'Us?'

'Myself and my companion.'

Again, she did not reply and Will continued, saying something inconsequential but dropping two or three passwords into the remark. If she was part of the network, she would recognise them. If not, she would soon dismiss him, considering him far too forward for a servant. Still she held his gaze.

My God, she is beautiful!

Slowly, she lowered her glass and put it down carefully on the table in front of her. Then she replied, praising the food he had brought and saying how hungry she was but this time, she inserted several words into the sentence which he recognised.

For a long moment neither of them spoke.

She is waiting for me to reveal myself.

Will swallowed. He would have to risk it. He had so little time. He dropped to one knee beside her chair and took one of her hands in his.

'I have been sent by John Reeves,' he whispered. And then she *did* react, turning towards him, her eyes wide.'

'What are you doing here, Mademoiselle?' he went on. 'You must be in mortal danger in this household.'

She did not reply directly but leant forward and said urgently. 'What is your true name, soldier?'

'Will Fraser.' She showed no recognition so he continued. 'The brother of Jack Fraser.'

She leant back in her chair then and sighed. 'Poor man. He did not deserve his fate.'

'You knew him?'

'Not personally, but I know Reeves trusted him.' Then she went on, her words tumbling over one another in her haste. 'You cannot linger here but we must talk more. Can you deliver a message for me? I can trust no one here and whenever I leave the house, de Menou insists on accompanying me, or that a member of his staff does so. She shuddered. He is like a slobbering dog, fawning over me all the time.' She sighed. 'I deliberately inserted myself into this household to eavesdrop and gather information and I have had to pretend an attraction for the man but ye gods, it is a heavy penance. I had prayed that Bayard would come last night so that I could pass a note to him even if it meant revealing ...'

'Revealing?'

She lowered her eyes. 'I have said too much,' she muttered. 'It is a veritable prison here and it is such a relief to speak with someone who is working for our cause. I ...'

Will interrupted her. He was still kneeling beside her, looking intently into her eyes and he felt very sure, then, that he knew her true identity. He picked his words with care for he sensed she needed more from him before she would admit it.

'I know that Gaston is a woman,' he said quietly, not dropping his gaze.

She continued to stare at him. Her body was utterly still and her eyes watchful and suspicious.

'Reeves told us.'

Still she did not move but her eyes narrowed. 'Us?' she whispered.

'My companion on this mission.'

She admitted nothing so Will pressed her further.

'You are Gaston, are you not, Mademoiselle?'

She shook off his hand and leapt to her feet, going to stand at the back of her chair and facing Will. Her expression was defiant and her shoulders tensed but then, of a sudden, she relaxed.

'Only Reeves knows,' she said. 'Apart from a trusted member of my own household – and one member of my family.'

And then, suddenly Will realised why her face and figure were familiar.

He smiled at her. 'Would that family member be a young widow with a chateau near Granville. The friend of a Catholic priest?'

'You have met my sister?'

'Only very briefly. But you closely resemble one another.'

She nodded. 'Blanche is helping our cause in a different way and she is constantly in danger herself.' Then she looked towards the door. 'I have discovered much during the last weeks and I need to pass on the information with all urgency otherwise lives will be lost and others uncovered.'

She paused. 'I dare not send a note by one of De Menou's servants. He knows royalists are baying for his blood and he inspects any correspondence that leaves this house. He has the eyes of a hawk.'

'You can trust me, Mademoiselle.'

She met his eyes. 'Yes, Will Fraser,' she said quietly. 'Yes, I believe I can.' Then she went on. 'Last night I discovered more vital information.' She grinned suddenly. 'I have developed the art of lip reading and become quite expert at interpreting whispered conversations. De Menou revealed much when he was in close conversation with Fouché.'

'You play a dangerous game, Mademoiselle.'

'Please, call me Catherine. And there is no need to remind me of my precarious situation. I pray that I shall soon be able to leave this place and return home in safety. She rose from her chair. 'Now go back to your duties and make sure it is you who comes to fetch my tray. I will have a note ready and tell you where to take it.'

On impulse, Will took her hand and kissed it then he let it drop and strode to the door where he paused and looked back. She was still looking at him.

'I am glad you are here, Will.'

He could not read the expression on her face.

Will ran down the stairs to the kitchen and resumed his duties but his mind was elsewhere.

My God, she must have steel nerves. If she is discovered, de Menou will show her no mercy.

He had not been in the kitchen more than fifteen minutes when he noticed that the butler was limping along the passage and heading for the stairs. Will jumped up and intercepted him. 'Shall I save you a climb, sir? I can fetch the lady's tray.'

'Oh, thank you, Etienne. Your legs are younger than mine.'

Will smiled and walked past him. He was aware that the butler was watching him from below so he paused at the top, straightened his clothes, put a hand through his hair and then turned left and knocked on the lady's door.

'Come!' Her voice held a distinct note of irritation and Will was instantly alert. He turned the handle and entered, seeing at once that she was not alone. De Menou was in the room.

Catherine's colour was heightened and they were staring at one another across the fireplace, de Menou's arm resting on the mantelpiece as he leant towards her.

Keeping his expression neutral and subservient and his eyes downcast, Will coughed discreetly. 'May I take your tray, Mademoiselle?'

It seemed she hardly noticed him. It was de Menou who replied.

'Yes, take it away and be quick about it.'

In the silence that followed, Will picked up the tray and walked quietly to the door. He could feel de Menou's eyes following his progress.

Once he was back in the kitchen he resumed polishing the silver but his hands were shaking. As casually as he could, he remarked to the butler that the Master had returned early from his dinner appointment.

'Yes, and in a rare bad mood, too,' he said. 'It appears that the evening was not enjoyable.'

'I'm sorry to hear that.'

The butler shrugged. 'He and his friends are jumpy now that Napoleon is in Paris. There's always the worry that the royalists might be brewing some plot. It may be the Master's heard some rumour or other.'

Will just nodded in response and continued with his work but his thoughts were focussed on how he could find a way of seeing Catherine and delivering her note. It would be foolhardy to go to her room again without a reason.

But he had reckoned without her ingenuity. Some time later, he heard de Menou descend the stairs, call for brandy and walk through the salon and towards the back of the house. And a few minutes later, Catherine came down the stairs holding a candelabra. The candles within it were worn down to stubs, though they had been tall and burning brightly when Will was in her room. She did not look at him but asked one of the other servants to replace the stubs and bring it back to her.

'It could use a polish, too,' she said.

Catherine turned on her heel and headed for the stairs. One of the maids busied herself replacing the candles. She was about to take it up when Will said. 'Let me give that candelabra a polish for the lady; she's right, the silver is badly tarnished.'

He took his time to give it a thorough polish and then stood up. He made to give it to the maid who was sitting on a stool, yawning, then he smiled at her. 'You look all in. I'll take it to the lady,' he said.

When Catherine opened the door, she pulled him inside.

'My God, Will,' she said. 'We must act fast. De Menou was in a fury just now. When I tried to calm him he spluttered something about damn royalists and a plot to assassinate the Emperor.'

'Is it true? Is there such a plot?'

Chapter Twenty-five

There was only a lone candle and that was over by her table near the fire, so he could not see her face clearly - but he saw her nod her head.

She moved towards the fire. 'Quick, bring the candelabra over here.'

He did as he was bid. She took a taper, put it to the fire and lit the new candles.

'All is in readiness,' she whispered. 'It has been months in the planning. Now Napoleon has returned to the capital we can put everything in place.'

'And now? Will you still go ahead with the plan?'

He saw that she was trembling and he held her shoulders. She looked up at him.

'De Menou let slip the name of one of the royalists they suspect. We thought that agent was safe, had not been uncovered. If he has that name, he will have others and he and Fouché's men will be seeking them out as we speak.'

Will frowned. 'I understood that your remaining agents were not suspected, that Reeves had recruited them himself?'

She shook her head. 'That is what we believed but now … now it seems every one of us may be in danger.'

'Even you?'

'I cannot tell, Will, but this has turned everything on its head. If Fouché has even a whiff of suspicion that I am involved, he'll not hesitate to arrest me.'

Will released her shoulders. 'This note,' he said. 'You have it ready?'

She nodded and took the note out from between her breasts. Will gave a wry smile.

She returned his smile but, even in the candlelight he could see that she was deadly pale.

'Should I take it to Bayard?'

She shook her head. 'The journey will take you too long. One of my trusted agents lives closer.' She told him the address and made him repeat it to her.

'Do you know the street?'

'No.'

Quickly, she gave him directions. 'Hurry, Will. Lives will depend on you getting there before Fouché's men.'

'What will your agent do?'

'He will alert all involved and tell them to go into hiding.' She swallowed. 'It may be that they are not all suspected but we cannot take risks.'

Will took the note and thrust it deep into the pocket of his shirt.

'I'm on my way.'

She followed him to the door. 'Godspeed,' she whispered.

Pausing only to excuse himself from the kitchen duties on grounds of tiredness, Will hurried out into the yard and into the tack room. The other men there were preparing for sleep and Armstrong sat alone in the corner. As Will entered, he got up and sauntered over. Will put an arm round his shoulders and led him back outside.

'We have a mission,' he whispered. 'Go back inside and fetch our coats. The men know you cannot answer them if they ask questions. And hurry, for the love of God.'

Armstrong didn't need telling twice. He hurried back into the room, grabbed their coats, grunted in reply to the ribald remarks from the other workers, and was back outside in no time.

When they were out of earshot, he whispered. 'They think we are going whoring.'

'I do not care what they think. We must make haste, Duncan.'

Once they were away from the house, striding as fast as possible along the dark streets, Will gave a brief, breathless account of what they were to do, and why.

'God, sir, we must pray we don't cross paths with Fouché's men.'

The night was pitch dark and there was a stillness in the air that presaged snow; not many people were abroad to hamper their progress.

Although Will thought he had memorised the route, he found that he had taken a wrong turn and they wasted precious time getting back on the right track, but at last, they saw the street name.

'It is at the other end from here,' said Will.

They walked as fast as they dared, not wanting to draw attention to themselves by running.

'It should be just after the bend,' whispered Will.

They found the house at last and Will hammered on the door, looking up and down the street as he did so.'

No one answered.

'All abed, I'll wager,' said Armstrong.

Will knocked again and stood back to listen. He frowned. 'I think there is some movement within,' he said.

'Maybe the fellow thinks it is Fouché's men.'

Will was about to knock again when he hesitated. 'Stay here, Duncan. There's an alley running alongside the house. I'll try and gain access to the back.'

'What shall I do if someone comes to the front door?'

Will gave him the name of the fellow and the code word. 'Make sure he identifies himself, then say the code word and if he answers correctly, tell him you have come from Gaston.'

Armstrong nodded in the darkness. 'Have a care, sir.'

'And you, Duncan. You have your dagger?'

Armstrong took it from his belt. 'At the ready, sir.'

Will crept down the alleyway. It was very narrow and the stench of urine and rotting vegetation made his eyes water. There was no light and an eerie quietness as if the city were holding its breath waiting for an impending snowfall. Will had to feel his way along the brickwork until he came to a small wooden door in the wall. The door was bolted but when he pushed at it he felt that it was not robust so he leant against it with all his strength and it gave way.

To his ears, the sound of splintering wood was deafening and he was sure he would have awakened the household. He unsheathed his short sword and felt his way down an overgrown path towards where he thought the back entrance must be.

The path led up to the back of the building, not seen in the pitch darkness, but only sensed. Will stopped, raised his hand and banged on the door.

Still there was no response. He stood completely still and listened. Still nothing. But then there was the smallest movement. So small that it could have been just a scuttling animal in the undergrowth but it alerted every nerve in his body and he whipped round.

And as he did so, a hand was clamped around his neck and he was forced back against the chest of his assailant. A voice hissed in his ear.

'Make one movement, my friend, and you are dead.'

Will's heart was racing and in the rush of fear, for a moment he forgot the code words and there were a few seconds when he stood helpless, the grip round his neck tightening.

'Who are you and what in God's name are you doing here?'

The words were still whispered and now he could feel a weapon pressed into his back.

He swallowed and then, mercifully, the code words floated back into his memory and haltingly, he repeated them.

He felt the grip loosen somewhat then and he took some breaths, waiting for a response, praying that he had established himself as a friend.

Though if he is not a friend, the words will mean nothing to him.

There was a beat of silence and then Will was spun round. It was so dark that he could not see his attacker's face but by his stance, he knew that he had a weapon in his hand.

Then the weapon was slowly lowered.

'Who has sent you?'

'Gaston.'

There was no reply.

'I beg you, sir, to listen to me. You have been betrayed. We know not by whom but I have it on good authority that Joseph Fouché has your name as a royalist supporter.

Will had expected some reaction but the man still did not move.

'Gaston never sends messengers.'

'I know, sir. But believe me, there was no time to take a note to a drop off point. It is a matter of great urgency, sir. You need to flee. Fouché's men may be on their way to arrest you.'

The man seemed to be considering this.

157

He still does not trust me.

'I have a note for you about my person. If you permit me to show it to you.'

The man stood back. 'Show it to me,' he said gruffly.

Will fumbled in his shirt, conscious that he was being keenly observed, and handed it over.

'I need light. Come inside with me while I read it.' He pushed Will in front of him towards the door and once inside the house, he lit a candle. Will stood silent as he did so. At last the man looked up. He tapped the note with his hand.

'It is genuine,' he said. 'I recognise the hand.'

'Then I beg you. Save yourself.'

He nodded. 'I have heard rumours,' he said quietly. 'And we have been much concerned about Gaston. No one has heard from him for weeks.'

'Gaston is safe,' said Will. 'For now.'

'You know his identity?'

Will nodded.

'Then you are the only one of us who does.'

'It is by not revealing his identity that he has kept safe. But please, sir, make haste. Warn your companions and leave directly.'

The man nodded. 'I am alone here. I have sent my household elsewhere for their safety. I will leave immediately. My instructions are in the note. I know where to go.'

He put the note to the candle flame and they both watched it burn.

Will breathed out. 'I will leave you to get ready,' he began. And then they both started. There was a frantic knocking on the back door and a shout.

'Sir! Open up for God's sake!'

Will headed for the door and the man tried to stop him but Will shook him off.

'It is my companion. He has been keeping watch at the front of the house.'

Armstrong burst in. 'A group of armed men are coming this way,' he said. 'For the love of God, make yourself scarce.'

Will stared at Armstrong. 'Fouché's men?'

'I didn't stop to ask!'

Will turned to the man. 'My companion and I will divert them,' he said. 'We'll leave from the front and start running. They will follow us and you can escape from the back.'

There was a slight hesitation.

'Do as I say,' said Will. 'We are British soldiers. We know how to defend ourselves. Hurry, man.'

The man stared at them. 'I ...'

'Go! Now! Before it is too late.'

He nodded. 'May God go with you.'

He went out of the back and was soon swallowed up by the darkness. Will snatched up the candle and he and Armstrong headed for the front of the house, thrusting it open and spilling out into the street.

Armstrong was right. The group of men were almost upon the house.

Will set off in the opposite direction, closely followed by Armstrong. Behind them they heard shouts. 'Give chase!'

Chapter Twenty-Six

Le Tréport

Blanche was exhausted. Neither she nor her coachman had had much sleep, breaking the journey only twice, at hostelries, to rest the horses and have a little food and sleep themselves.

'You're mighty impatient to reach your destination, Madame,' said the coachman, yawning and stretching as he harnessed up the horses for the last day's travel.'

Blanche didn't answer but lowered her eyes from his curious gaze.

The coachman chuckled.

Let him think what he pleases. If he spreads a rumour that I have a lover in this region, tongues will wag, but that is all. As long as I am not suspected of other activities.

As the coach slithered down the hill towards the main street of the town of Le Tréport, Blanche opened the window and gazed up at the towering chalk cliffs above. She glanced at the ruins of the great Abbey of St Michel which had seen centuries of monastic life.

What a history it has had, this little fishing port.

The coachman brought the pair of horses to a halt on the main street which ran along the sea front and Blanche stepped down. As he was getting her bag, she gazed back toward the cliffs. It was here, in between the high cliffs and the pebble beach, that the mouth of the river Bresle met the English Channel.

'This do for you Madame?'

She smiled. She never let him know where she went in the town but just asked to be put down anywhere along the front.

'It will do very well,' she said.

Blanche thanked him warmly for his trouble.

'Will I put up somewhere local until you are ready to journey home, Madame?'

She shook her head. 'Not this time,' she said. 'I do not know how long I shall stay.' She hesitated. 'I have friends in the region who will bring me safely back.'

Then she pressed some coin into his hand. 'No need to hurry on the journey home. Take your time and see that you do not strain either yourself or the horses.'

He doffed his cap and heaved himself back into the driver's seat, turned the carriage and headed back the way they had come. Blanche stood watching the departing coach and when it was out of sight she picked up her bag and walked briskly down the street until she came to a chandler's shop, with its distinctive sign of a cast iron ship swinging above the entrance.

Blanche knocked lightly on the door. The knock was answered immediately by an elderly woman who looked out anxiously, scanning the street before ushering her in, then saying, in a low voice, 'Is there trouble?'

Blanche moved forward and took the woman's hands. 'Nothing we've not faced before, Madame. Do not fret. Is Jean-Paul at home?'

Just at that moment a man's voice greeted her and she saw a familiar figure approach, picking his way through the mass of goods for sale – everything for use on board a boat or ship; ropes, lines, hawsers, anchors, buoys and much else besides.

'Le Petit Matelot!' he said, smiling. 'It is not often that we see you in your normal attire!' He drew her inside and closed the door. 'You have new instructions?' he said softly.

Blanche nodded. Then the old woman interrupted. 'Where are my manners! You will be cold and hungry after your journey. Come, there is a merry fire burning within and I will fetch you food and drink from the kitchen.'

When she had bustled off, Jean-Paul put her bag at the foot of the stairs then escorted Blanche into the back room. He settled her into a chair by the fire and pulled up another close to her. 'What is the news?'

'I have intelligence from England,' she said quietly. 'It appears that one of Reeves' newly recruited agents has been uncovered and if one is known to Fouché's men it may mean …'

'It may mean they suspect others.'

'Indeed. And also …'

161

'Also?'

'There is still no news of Gaston. It is feared that he may be being kept prisoner.'

Jean-Paul rubbed his chin. 'That is grave news indeed. Without Gaston at its head, the Paris network will be in disarray.' He frowned. 'So, what is the plan? Are you to alert your sailor friends?'

At that moment, the old woman came into the room bearing a bowl of hot chocolate which was placed on the table beside Blanche's chair. She took a sip, smiled and declared it delicious, then waited until she had left the room.

'I would not alarm your mother,' she said quietly. Then she continued.

'Because Napoleon has recently returned, Fouché's men are on high alert. Whenever he is in the capital they fear he is vulnerable to attack by royalists.'

Jean-Paul smiled grimly. 'They have good reason to be suspicious, do they not?'

Blanche took a long draught of her drink. 'Of course. Always.' She hesitated. 'Particularly now.'

There was a pregnant silence.

'And you are not going to divulge any more intelligence?'

She put down her bowl carefully and looked up at him. 'I have only been told what I need to know,' she said.

'And what is that?'

She told him of the galley expected into Le Tréport on the 14th of February.

'A galley? You don't see them often these days. It will be remarked upon.'

Blanche shrugged. 'This vessel has been used for such operations before and is regularly used for trading purposes. I'm told it is not such an unusual sight in these waters.'

'I suppose it has the advantage of oars if the wind is not set fair.'

'And it can take a good many passengers.'

'How many are you expecting?'

Blanche shrugged. 'I do not know. But there are likely to be many more than usual and it will be my job to make sure they are not suspected by prying eyes.'

'And smooth their journey to the coast no doubt?'

She sighed. 'Indeed. In Beauvais, as you know, there is a safe house well established and our contact there has an estate outside the town where many of our royalist friends can be concealed, but in the towns between Beauvais and the coast, this will not be so easy.' She looked up at him. 'They have put up one or two fleeing to the coast in the past but never more.'

'You can rely on me,' said Jean-Paul. I will send word to alert our friends in these places and tell them to expect more folk than usual and to prepare places where they can rest and hide.'

'They will not expect luxury.'

'They will not find it. I am thinking of sheds and outhouses and abandoned buildings.'

She nodded, then put her hand on his arm. 'You are a good friend, Jean-Paul.'

He smiled. 'And you, Madame, are a brave woman. And,' he continued. 'I look forward to seeing you dressed in your sailor clothes once more. I imagine you have brought them with you?'

'Of course'

'Le Petit Matelot.'

'Indeed.'

Jean-Paul rose. 'Come, I'll take you to your room. You must rest tonight and tomorrow we will set about laying our plans.'

Blanche followed him up the stairs and he opened the door into a small bedroom where a fire had hastily been lit for her. As he turned to go, she said. 'There is one other thing.'

'And what is that?'

She frowned and chewed at her nail. 'I think it is possible that I myself may be under suspicion.'

Then, in low tones, she told him about the young swordsman who had been found lurking in Father Jacques' woods.

'Have you any idea who he is?'

She shook her head. 'None.' She shrugged. 'And it may be that he was not spying on me at all.'

Jean-Paul came over and took her shoulders. 'You must take every care, my dear. If anything should befall you ...'

'I do take every care, my friend. I told my household that I was leaving for Paris.'

Early the next morning, Blanche left the house with Jean-Paul. She was no longer the woman of quality wearing a fashionable travelling cloak but as her other persona, Le Petit Matelot. She was dressed in a well-worn blue shirt with a turned-down collar, a wide jacket and loose trousers with faded blue white and red stripes. She had pinned up her hair and crammed it into a woollen cap which she wore pulled down low. Her face and her hands were streaked with grime.

To those who did not know her, her backstory was convincing though, if any chose to go into it in depth, it would not stand scrutiny. She was a boy sailor, crew of a gunship patrolling the coast, on a few days' shore leave, staying with her uncle, the chandler. It gave her the ability to move freely in the little port and meet with trusted royalists among the sea going community, alerting them to the imminent arrival of their colleagues who had been uncovered and needed to leave the country with all haste.

She could not know how many had been discovered, nor when they would arrive or whether they would all come together or separately. All she could do was to get into conversation with her own contacts, alert them to the arrival of La Belle on the 14th of February and eavesdrop on conversations between sailors, sea captains and the fishing community, gathering as much useful information as she could.

Meanwhile, Jean-Paul and her own contacts would gather suitable clothing together to disguise the refugees so that they did not stand out as strangers.

All those fleeing would identify themselves through code words. The hosts at their last safe house would give them new ones and tell them how to contact Le Petit Matelot.

She was exhausted by the time she arrived back at the chandler's shop and was very grateful for the meal served to her by his mother. Jean-Paul was not there when she arrived but he came in later and out of his mother's hearing, they exchanged information about what arrangements they had both made.

As she rose from the table to go up to bed, she turned to him.

'Jean-Paul?'

'Madame.'

'Are you certain that all your contacts can be trusted?'

He frowned. 'As certain as I can be,' he said slowly. 'But, as you know, enemies can infiltrate even the most solid network. Cast your mind back to the man de Menou. He was trusted implicitly by the British Government, was he not?'

'Indeed.' She hesitated then smiled at him. 'Bonsoir, Jean-Paul. And thank you.'

He took her hand and kissed it. 'Mon petit Matelot.'

Even though she ached in every limb, sleep did not come quickly that night and Blanche eventually rose and lit the candle again. The bare boards were cold beneath her feet as she walked over to the little window set in the eaves and looked out. There was a thin crescent moon and it was not so inky black tonight. The town was silent and only the constancy of the waves on the beach pulling at the pebbles disturbed the silence.

She shivered and made her way back to her bed. She did not extinguish the candle straight away but watched the flickering shadows it made on the walls.

And when, at last, sleep claimed her it was not peaceful. Images of a young swordsman flitted in and out of her dreams and once she awoke, having to stifle a scream as she dreamt he had found her and was raising his sword to strike.

Chapter Twenty-Seven

Paris

Will and Armstrong ran for their lives.

'Where to, sir?'

'Anywhere,' panted Will. 'We'll have to shake them off.'

They rounded the corner and for a few moments they were out of the sight of their pursuers. They raced down the next alley which led off the main street.

'Pray God there is a way out of here,' muttered Armstrong as he ran, then in front of him, Will skidded to a halt.

'In here.'

Armstrong could see nothing but he followed Will, squeezing himself through a narrow gap in a broken wall. They both squatted down behind it, breathing hard.

'If they find us here at least it will be easy to defend,' whispered Will,' and Armstrong nodded into the darkness.

As they crouched there surrounded by the smell of rotting vegetation and human excrement, they heard the sounds of a city settling for the night, all around them. The occasional shout of laughter, or of abuse, of doors being bolted, lights extinguished but then the relative silence was punctuated by another sound, the pounding of boots on cobbled streets, close by, now, shaking the place awake again.

'How many men did you see, Duncan?'

Armstrong shrugged. 'Didn't stop to count, sir. Maybe twenty.'

'Armed?'

'I saw swords. 'Course they may have pistols, too. I didn't wait to find out.'

'Aye. You did well to warn us so quickly.'

'Do you reckon he'll get away, that royalist fellow?'

'There's a good chance.'

They said nothing more but listened intently. Then a shouted order from one of the men. 'Search the alleyways. They'll have crept down one of them for sure, the stinking rats.'

The group had stopped now and it seemed that their leader was giving them instructions. Will and Armstrong could hear muttered

166

conversation floating through the night air down from the main street. And then further sounds of boots on cobbles, all going in different directions.

Voices came closer now. There were men coming down their alley, speaking together in low voices. Will and Armstrong couldn't judge how many but it didn't sound as though there were more than two or three.

They stayed utterly still, holding their breath. Then they heard the men pass the gap they'd squeezed through earlier and go further down the alley. Armstrong tapped Will on the shoulder.

'I reckon we're safe. We just need to stay here until they give up the search and then ...' he began. But his words were interrupted by a shout from further down the alley.

'There's no way through. It's a dead end.'

'Good of them to let us know,' whispered Will.

They waited and, before long they heard the searchers coming back and walking up the alley towards the main street. They were talking in low tones, too quiet for Will and Armstrong to catch their words, but it seemed they had decided that no fugitives could be concealed in a dead-end alley and when they had passed the gap in the wall Will shifted his position slightly and relaxed. He was about to whisper to Armstrong when one of the men stopped. Then there was some more muttering.

'I didn't see no gap. What are you talking about, man?'

More muttered conversation, then the men retraced their steps and stopped right outside the broken wall.

'Nah! They'd not be able to squeeze through there. You try if you care to but I reckon you'll get stuck half way.'

Armstrong made the slightest movement to get his dagger to the front of his body. Will's short sword was already drawn. But as soon as the man's head came through the gap, Will grasped it round the neck and jerked it fiercely while Armstrong put his hand over the man's mouth to silence him. From the outside, all his companion could see was the death throes of convulsing legs.

'Told you you'd get stuck, you great fool,' he said. Then he started to drag his companion out, laughing and passing comments all the while.

Will and Armstrong were ready. The moment the man's body

flopped out of the hole and landed inert on the ground, they waited while his friend kneeled down beside him.

'What ails you, yer great ...'

But he didn't have a chance to say more. Will was through the gap and onto him at once, a hand over his mouth and his sword thrust through his heart. The man's head slumped and he keeled over onto the ground.

'Is he gone?' whispered Armstrong.

'Yes,' said Will shortly. 'And soon their companions will come looking for them.'

He started to drag one of the dead men further down the alley and Armstrong followed his lead and did the same with the other one. 'How far, sir?' he panted.

'To the end, Duncan. As far as possible from our hiding place.'

They dumped the two bodies by a wall at the end of the alley and then crept back and through the gap to their hiding place.

'What now?' asked Armstrong.

'We haven't much time,' said Will. 'Their friends will know they came this way. We can't stay here in case we are discovered.'

'This darned darkness. There's not even a bloody moon to help us, sir.'

'We've been in tighter spots before, Duncan.'

'But if we can't see where we are going ...'

Armstrong felt his way forward in the dark. The ground was rough and overgrown with brambles but he pushed on. 'There's another wall here, sir,' he said, as he saw a dark solid shape looming up in the darkness ahead.

'Then we'll have to climb it.'

'Where are we sir, do you think?'

'In the back yard of someone's house.'

Armstrong missed his footing and lay spread-eagled in a tangle of thorns. He swore as he righted himself and sucked the blood from his hand.

'So it's up and over, is it, sir, until we find a way out?'

Will grinned into the darkness. 'All I can think of, Duncan,' he whispered.

'And have you any idea how to get back to de Menou's place?'

'No.'

Chapter Twenty-Eight

Near Granville

Blanche's maid, Suzanne, had hardly slept. She was worried about her mistress, journeying North up the coast through the night but even more worried about the task entrusted to her. Would she find the drop off point in the village which Madame had specified? She knew she could confide in no one.

She rose before dawn, dressed in her warmest clothes and stoutest shoes and put the package Blanche had given her at the bottom of the canvas bag she had provided, together with a few travel essentials. Then she went down to the kitchen where a yawning kitchen maid was stoking the fire. She gave Suzanne a bowl of chocolate and the food the cook had made up for her journey the night before.

'Going to visit your family, Suzanne? That's a fair way.'

Suzanne nodded, peering out of the window as she drank. 'It'll be light soon. I'll be on my way,' she said.

'Where's the mistress off to this time?'

'Paris.'

'All right for some. What I would give to see Paris.'

Suzanne didn't answer but drained her bowl quickly and then headed for the door.

It was bitterly cold and an Easterly wind had got up. Suzanne pulled her cloak more securely round her and slung the canvas bag over her shoulder and across her chest. From Blanche's house she took a shortcut through the woods and into Father Jacque's property, then down his drive turning South when she reached the road. She had only gone a few yards when she heard a slight movement and she stopped and peered into the trees, her sharp eyes picking out a tethered horse a little way off the road. She stood and stared at it and it jerked its head up and gave a soft whinny. She could see no fire or sign of human life, but there was a lingering smell of smoke on the wind. She frowned, knowing that the animal's owner must be close by but she could see no sign

169

of movement in the semi darkness. Her heart beating a little faster, she quickened her step, tightened her grip on her bag and walked on.

'Just some traveller,' she told herself but as she plodded on she felt discomforted by the thought. Several times she looked back until the outline of the horse became indistinct, then she turned the corner and it was lost to sight.

But its rider had been awake and alert. He had seen Blanche's coach leave in the night and turn North and was waiting until light to report this to his handler. And when the young girl had appeared from the drive, he could not be sure but he thought he recognised her as Blanche de Valois' maid. He had watched her scuttle away in the opposite direction.

Slowly he stretched his stiff limbs and rubbed at his leg. The wound was healing but it was still mighty sore. His fingers were cold and his movements awkward as he rummaged in his saddle bag for the food he had brought with him.

The girl was going his way so he would follow her, but there was no need to hurry; he would catch her up when it was fully light.

Chapter Twenty-Nine

Paris

Will and Armstrong had hauled themselves over walls, through yards and along a muddle of dark alleyways, often missing their foothold in the dark and falling or tripping, muffling their curses. Once or twice they stopped and listened. Not long after they had left their hiding place, there was a shout.

'They have found the bodies,' whispered Armstrong, and Will nodded into the darkness. 'They'll know we can't get out of that alleyway. Won't be long before they're on our scent.'

They had climbed over a wall into yet another dark alleyway when Will stopped. 'There's a light there,' he whispered.

Armstrong stood beside him, panting. 'D'you reckon that's a proper street?'

'Only one way to find out,' said Will.

They crept up the alleyway to its entrance and peered out. There was no visible name on the street but there was no sign of their pursuers, either. The street's lights had been extinguished and the light they had seen came from an open doorway where a drunken man was haranguing a servant.

Keeping close to the wall, Will and Armstrong walked along the street, conscious of the noise of their every step. At length they came to a crossing.

'Which way now?'

Will shrugged into the darkness. 'I cannot tell, Duncan. But we need to get into some populated area where there is some night life, so we can melt into the crowd.'

Armstrong looked up at the sky. 'Not even a sodding star to guide us. Can't even tell the direction.'

'Take heart, Duncan. Fouché's men never saw us. They won't recognise us. If we can mingle with late night revellers, we shall be safe.'

But it was a full half-hour later when finally they spied light in the distance and drawn towards it as moths to a flame, they came upon an area they recognised and, better still, were able to mingle with a crowd of revellers who were calling for their coaches, shouting good night to one another or stumbling off into the Paris night. Will stopped to get his bearings.

Armstrong pointed. 'Place Vendome's over there, I reckon.'

'Well done Sergeant! We've led our enemies a merry dance. It seems we have come in a full circle.'

Greatly relieved, they made their way in the direction of de Menou's house and as they approached it, Armstrong nudged Will's arm.

'What's our story then, sir? Been whoring, have we?'

Will smiled. 'It's a story our companions will believe, at least.'

He was right. The next morning, their companions laughed and nudged each other, remarking how exhausted Will and Armstrong looked and neither of them denied that they had had a night of debauchery. But Will hardly noticed all the sly looks. He and Armstrong had had a whispered conversation earlier.

'I must speak to Catherine,' he said. 'She has to know her note has been delivered to her man and that Fouché's men were after him.'

'I fear the lady is in danger, sir. Do you believe she is under suspicion?'

Will rubbed his chin, unused to the thick beard that had grown there.

'I cannot tell. But the longer she stays in this house, the more likely it will be that it becomes the case.'

After the maid had delivered some refreshments to the workers mid-morning, Will gathered up the platters and took them into the kitchen. He lingered there as long as he dared trying to judge the mood of the house but all seemed as usual and the cook told him that some of the regular staff had recovered and were soon due back at work. He was about to make his way back into the yard when the butler came into the kitchen.

'Etienne,' he said, and for a moment Will forgot his pseudonym and failed to reply. 'Etienne,' he said again and this time Will turned towards him. 'I would speak with you,' he said.

Will followed the butler down the passage and into his room. He closed the door.

'I have not forgotten my promise, Etienne,' he said. 'If you can be patient, I will approach the Master and ask for you to be employed on the staff here, but just now ...' He cast his eyes to the door.

'Just now?'

'He is in a fearsome temper. It would not be a good moment.'

'I'm sorry to hear that, sir,' said Will. 'Do you know what ails him?'

The butler leaned in towards Will. 'Perhaps I should not tell you this, but the Chief of Police called in late last night, hammering on the door in a frightful rage, demanding that I rouse the Master.'

Will tried to keep his face expressionless but he could not help clenching his fist. 'Oh dear, sir, do you know what had happened?'

The butler hesitated. 'Well, when I took them some refreshment I did hear ...'

Will said nothing and the man continued. 'You know of these damn royalists?'

'Of course,' said Will. 'They are a threat to the Emperor, are they not.'

He nodded. 'It appears that there is another conspiracy but when Fouché's men went to round up the royalist conspirators last night, every one of them had fled.'

'The Minister of Police must be disappointed,' said Will.

'Disappointed! He was furious. And that fury has transferred itself to the Master. Why, he was ranting and raving earlier about suspecting someone in his own household for tipping them off.'

'No. Surely that could not be so?'

The butler shook his head. 'I am sure it is not but it has made every member of his household nervous.' He sighed. 'So you see, Etienne, this is not a moment to approach him about a new appointment.'

'I quite understand, sir.'

He excused himself and walked out into the yard, his mind in turmoil. It sounded to him as if the net was closing. He must warn Catherine.

Chapter Thirty

Near Granville

Suzanne was making good progress. It was fully light now and the threatened snow had not fallen but been dispersed by the wind. Now the sky was blue and cloudless and her spirits rose. She had not had leave to visit her family in over three months and she was looking forward to seeing her mother and father and her three younger siblings. Madame Blanche had given her little gifts for the children and some other treats for the family to add to the simple supplies in their cottage.

She kept up a steady pace and hummed a familiar tune to herself as she travelled, smiling as she did so, remembering her mother singing it to her when she was little.

Suzanne's mother had been Madame Blanche's nurse when she was a child and Blanche had loved her dearly; Blanche had been delighted when Suzanne herself had been old enough to enter her service. It was because of this connection that Madame trusted her with her secrets, even more, now, since the Master had died. Suzanne did not know where Blanche went, exactly, when she was away from home. She entertained in her house when she was in residence and the gentry of the region came and went and the place was full of merriment and she would be invited hither and thither. But then there were the secret times when she disappeared, sometimes for weeks at a time and Suzanne had to pack the rough sailor's outfits for her.

She was still beautiful, that was for sure, and the coachman was convinced she had a lover.

Suzanne *knew* she had a lover, but he was closer to home and she would never reveal his name to anyone. Let the rest of the household gossip and guess, but only she knew the truth.

It was still early but a few carts had passed her, laden with agricultural goods. A couple of carriages passed her too, travelling when they could in the short daylight hours, so she took little notice when she heard the sound of a horse trotting along behind her. She stood at the side of the road to let it pass but much to her surprise, the rider drew up alongside her. She looked up and saw a young man astride a bay mare.

'Bonjour Mademoiselle,' he said, putting his riding crop to his hat. 'Where are you headed?'

'I go to visit my family, sir.' And she named the village.

'Still some way to go. I am headed that way.' He patted the horse's rump. 'You can ride behind me if you like. It will give your legs a rest and you'll make faster progress.'

Suzanne looked horrified. 'Oh no, sir, I could not do that,' she said. 'I have never ridden on a horse in my life and besides …' she bit her lip.

He smiled down at her. 'I promise you that my intentions are honourable,' he said, 'And for the next few miles I intend to walk the horse, to rest her, the poor beast. We were delayed earlier and I rode her through the night. And I'd be glad of the company,' he added.

Suzanne thought back to the moment when she had turned onto the road and seen the tethered horse in the trees and smelt the smoke. She smiled to herself. How foolish she had been to take fright. There was an innocent explanation. She hesitated. Then he swung himself down from the saddle and she half laughed and half screamed as he lifted her off her feet and onto the mare's back. She had to admit that it was a relief to take the weight off her sore feet. The young man handed her the canvas bag.

'What have you got in there, young lady,' he said, laughing. 'It's mighty heavy.'

She didn't answer him but put the bag back over her shoulders. He mounted carefully and she noticed that one of his legs was stiff and seemingly pained him.

'Put your arms round my waist and hold on tightly,' he said.

She gasped as they set off with a jolt, but soon she got into the way of swaying to the horse's gait and began to relax.

He turned back to her from time to time, remarking on the weather or the countryside and occasionally asking her questions about herself. He seemed a polite young gentleman and she was glad that his body shielded her from the wind. She was weary from her restless night and walking with her heavy bag and, once or twice, she almost dozed off as she leant into him, the rhythm of the horse's stride making a repetitive beat in her head. She smiled to herself thinking of her mother's horror if she knew Suzanne had accepted a ride from the young gentleman.

Time slipped by and the sun was as high as it would reach when she saw the milepost.

'Sir, I shall get off here,' she said.

He brought the horse to a halt and turned to her. 'This is not the village you mentioned.'

'No, but I have a call to make here first.'

'Shall I wait for you while you make your call?'

'Oh no sir. I … I may be some time and I would not delay you. And it is no distance from here to my mother's house.'

He dismounted and helped her down.

'Thank you, sir. You have been very kind.'

'It was a pleasure to have your company,' he said, remounting with some difficulty.

'Does your leg pain you, sir?'

He shook his head. 'A fall from the horse a few days ago,' he said. 'It is nothing.'

But she saw the grimace of pain on his face.

He squeezed the mare's flanks and trotted down the road. For a few moments, Suzanne watched him, then she walked towards the village but, remembering Blanche's instructions, she then turned left up a cart track, frowning as she looked for the landmark she'd been given; the dead oak tree which stood out in the high hedges which lined the track. As she approached it, she looked round nervously but she was alone and out of sight. Feeling behind the tree she found the wide slit in the bark and stuffed the package inside. The squawk of a blackbird which flew out from the hedge made her jump and she looked around again but there was no sign of humanity. Quickly she walked away, back down the track and out onto the road towards her home, relieved that she had successfully carried out her mission.

But she *had* been observed. The young man had trotted briskly up the road but when he had gone a little way he turned and looked back, seeing the way Suzanne was heading. Then he went back the way he had come, not on the road but in amongst the trees that lined it. He watched her turn up the track and then he found a hiding place from where he could observe her. He saw her stop at the dead oak tree, feel around it, then withdraw a package from her bag.

He stayed where he was and waited until she had retraced her tracks and regained the road. Then he came out of his hiding place and rode up the track to the tree and withdrew the package. He stuffed it into his saddlebag, grinning. Gold for the royalists! Coming direct from Blanche de Valois.

Proof positive that she was a spy. His handler would be well pleased with him.

Chapter Thirty-One

Paris

As soon as he could, Will sought out Armstrong and they found a spot out of sight of the other workers where they could speak freely.

'I fear for Catherine,' whispered Will. 'Apparently de Menou is in a rage and suspects that someone in his own household is a royalist spy.'

'You think he'll work out who it is?'

Will nodded. 'I fear he may have made the connection. Catherine inveigling herself into his household, pretending affection for him but never letting him touch her, then Fouché dining here and Catherine observing him closely. De Menou is no fool. We must act quickly to get her away from Paris.'

'Have you a plan?'

Will shook his head. 'No plan, Duncan. We do not know which agents are now under suspicion, which have fled. Even she will not. All is in turmoil.'

'Then maybe we should go to Mass,' said Armstrong.

'What!'

'Is Father Jacques still in Paris?'

'Ah, I see your reasoning. I have no idea whether he is still here but there will be eyes everywhere. If we effect her escape from this house, someone will notice. There will be a hue and cry.'

One of their fellow workers walked past and hailed them.

'A night of whoring was it?'

Will shrugged. 'Soldiers take their pleasures where they can find them,' he said.

'And your wounded friend, too?'

'He may not be able to speak, but Pierre has other talents,' said Will.

Armstrong smirked and the man walked on, chuckling.

'What can I do?' asked Armstrong, once he was out of sight.

Will rubbed his head. 'I'll find a way to get to her. Meanwhile, collect our belongings and meet me on the street. But stay out of sight until I come.'

Will was about to go back into the house when Armstrong pulled at his sleeve. 'Fetch your firearm and your sword first.'

'I should not …'

'Be prepared, sir.'

Will nodded and slipped into the outhouse. All the other workers were employed elsewhere. He found the weapons where he had hidden them and concealed them about his person.

As he walked towards the house, the carpenter hailed him. 'Oy, Etienne. You're needed here.'

Will paused. 'Sorry, sir, I've been asked to do an errand for the Master. I'll be back soon.'

He darted into the kitchen. There was only one of the kitchen maids there. She was leaning over the sink peeling some vegetables. She blushed when she saw him and turned to speak to him but he forestalled her.

'Mademoiselle La Fargue has requested a drink of cordial,' he said.

Will the girl not question that I am wearing my work clothes for this?

With maddening slowness, the girl fetched a small tray and filled a glass. She put the glass on the tray.

'She has a liking for the little madeleines Cook bakes,' she said. 'There's a batch not long out of the oven. Wait while I fetch some.'

She seemed to take pleasure in keeping Will in the kitchen as long as possible and his every nerve was stretched as he expected to be challenged by the Cook or the Butler at any moment.

At last, all was prepared and he made his way to the foot of the stairs trying to keep slow and steady although every fibre of his being was alert.

He paused at Catherine's door and was about to knock when he heard voices from within.

De Menou!

There was no mistaking the voice. And it was raised in anger.

'You little bitch! You shall pay for this. My God I'll see you suffer!'

Then Catherine's voice, mollifying. 'My dear man, I have no notion of what you accuse me. I came here at your invitation and

I thought you cared for me.'

'Don't you *dare.*' There was a sharp intake of breath and a muffled scream.

My God, he's attacking her.

Catherine's voice again. 'Please. You are hurting me.'

'And I'm going to hurt you some more, ye gods I'm going to hurt you 'til you beg for mercy.'

Catherine's voice was less steady now. 'You asked me to be your *wife!*'

'You played me you little whore! You deceived me with your wiles. And all the time you were spying on me. You're nothing but a royalist cunt.'

Then there was the unmistakable sound of a slap, another cry of pain and of a body hitting the floor.

Will waited no longer. Without knocking, he came into the room and carefully put the tray down.

'You requested some cordial, Mademoiselle,' he said.

De Menou was aiming a kick at Catherine's prone body but he spun round as Will entered.

'Get out!' he yelled.

Will continued to stand there. As Catherine tried to struggle to her feet, de Menou aimed another kick at her, but Will was faster. He shot across the room and put his body in front of hers.

'That's no way to treat a lady,' he said calmly, but inside his fury and hatred were reaching boiling point.

De Menou took a step forward. 'Get out of my way, you low life!'

Will did not move and de Menou looked him full in the face, spluttering with rage. Then he pushed Will in the chest. 'Get out!' he repeated. And then, when Will still did not move, he pushed him again. 'How dare you disobey me! Who the hell do you think you are? Get out of my sight. Get out of my house!'

Still Will did not move. De Menou was very close to him now and Will was aware that Catherine had risen to her feet. For a moment, he wondered whether she was armed and whether, between them, they could hold de Menou at gunpoint, tie him up and gag him then make their escape. But then he saw de Menou reach down towards his belt.

The man wasn't quick enough. Before his hand had even made contact with the top of his dagger, Will had his wrist in a vice-like grip. De Menou was not a fighting man, he was bloated with good living and he was no match for the soldier in front of him. Will pulled his wrist up and forced it behind his back and then pinned him against the wall.

De Menou gasped with pain as Will loomed over him. He tried to cry out, tried to call for someone to come to his aid, but Catherine had anticipated this and she was already there, her hand clamped over the man's slobbering mouth.

De Menou's eyes were bulging and it was then that Will saw the naked fear in his eyes.

'You asked who I am, sir. Do you not know me?'

De Menou tried to shake his head and continued to stare at Will and then, suddenly, Will saw the flicker of recognition in his eyes. Not recognition for a servant in his household but for another man, a man from his past.

'My name is Fraser.'

De Menou bit down on Catherine's hand. She gasped and lost her grip.

'Fraser is dead,' he managed to spit out before Catherine had recovered herself and replaced her hand.

'Apparently not,' said Will. 'As you see.'

Then with all his strength, de Menou suddenly flung himself against Catherine and sent her sprawling. Will's instinct was to go to her aid and if his reactions had not been those of a soldier, he might have been distracted, for she had fallen hard. But he was fully focussed on the man in front of him. He saw de Menou's hand reaching for his weapon again and this time Will did not hesitate. He drew his sword in an instant and plunged it into de Menou's heart.

'This is for my brother,' he hissed, as it struck home.

It was so quick and so accurate that de Menou's only expression was one of surprise and he slumped to the floor, clutching his chest, the blood spewing from his mouth.

Catherine rose slowly to her feet and for a few minutes, she and Will stood, frozen, as they watched de Menou gurgle and twitch and then finally lie still as the life drained from him.

Then Will turned away with a shudder and sheathed his sword, his fury spent. He went to Catherine and put his hands on her shoulders. He could feel that she was trembling and the blow she'd received on the cheek was already an angry red. She took a deep breath and swallowed as she gazed at the lifeless figure on the floor.

'Don't look,' he said.

'I have seen death before,' she said. 'When I was a child; my family … at the time of the Terror. It brings it back. You never forget.'

Will didn't reply.

She looked up then. 'Well, Will Fraser,' she said quietly. 'It seems that you and I must become fugitives.'

He nodded. 'I'm sorry.'

'Sorry? What are you sorry for?'

'That I have brought you to this.'

'He had already uncovered me, Will. My fate would have been a deal worse if you had not come when you did.'

She sighed. 'I admit that I am fearful, though. As soon as de Menou's body is discovered …'

She did not need to spell out the consequences. She looked up at him. 'My contacts are dispersed and as soon as it is known that I have fled, Fouché and his men will be after me.'

'I have a plan,' said Will, slowly. 'It is ill formed but it is the best I can devise.'

'Then tell me. For I have none.'

Will gave a weak smile. 'We shall go to Mass.'

'For what reason? To atone for our sins?'

Quickly, he whispered his plan to her. 'It's all we can think of for the moment.'

She nodded. 'At least it is a plan – and it will suffice for now.'

She went to the armoire and quickly took out a few possessions, concealing some about her person and putting others into a bag, with a last look at de Menou's lifeless body, they left the room. Catherine was dressed in a travelling cloak with a cowl and she pulled it close to disguise her sore face. Then she took the key from the inside, closed the door and locked it from the outside.

Catherine walked slowly down the stairs, followed at a

respectful distance by Will. When they reached the kitchen, the cook had returned. Forestalling any questions, Catherine smiled at her.

'Vicomte de Menou has asked Etienne to escort me to my house,' she said. 'I have some orders to give there and some things to collect.'

'Very good, Mademoiselle.' She paused. 'I hope you enjoyed the madeleines.'

Just for a second, Catherine looked confused but then she quickly recovered her composure.

'They were delicious. Some of your very best.'

'Thank you, Mademoiselle.'

'I shall be back by evening.'

'Very good, Mademoiselle.'

They made their way out into the yard and found the carpenter.

'I'm sorry to take him away from his work,' said Catherine. 'But Vicomte de Menou has asked Etienne here to accompany me to my house.'

'Very good Mademoiselle,' said the carpenter. 'Is your mute friend to go with you,' he asked, turning to Will.

'Yes, I fear he is,' said Catherine, before Will could reply. 'I have some heavy work for him.'

'I'll make it up to you,' said Will, knowing that he would never see the man again.

'Hm. See that you do.'

Out in the street, Armstrong emerged from where he had concealed himself. He was carrying two haversacks and Will immediately relieved him of one.

They started walking away from de Menou's house as rapidly as they dared, dodging the mud and the horse manure, until Catherine spotted a one horse fiacre a little way ahead, its yellow numbers stark against the black hood, and Armstrong ran to secure its services.

As they climbed up onto the seat behind the driver and directed him to take them to Notre Dame on the Ile de la Cité, Will looked back.

How long will it be before de Menou is discovered?

Chapter Thirty-Two

They squeezed up together on the seat and were bounced along the streets towards the 4th arrondissement and the Île de la Cité. They spoke little on the journey, but Will clasped Catherine's hand and held it firm. She did not withdraw it, but when they reached the bridge over the River Seine and were waiting to cross it, she gave a shudder as they saw the great cathedral looming up in front of them with its twin towers and flying buttresses.

'I have never been inside,' she said. 'It holds too many memories.'

'Memories?'

'When I was young, my father told me how the cathedral had been ransacked and nearly destroyed during the 90's.'

'During the Terror? You said your family suffered.'

She nodded. 'They suffered terribly, but now is not the time to speak of it.'

'Pray God I can keep you safe,' he muttered.

She smiled up at him. 'I am used to danger, Will. And we are both resourceful.'

They travelled over the bridge and past rows of empty stalls where the newly established flower market happened in the Spring and Summer. Now the place was silent and deserted.

As they approached the cathedral, Armstrong cleared his throat and leant forward. 'What if we cannot find Father Jacques? What if he has left? What if nothing is known of him?'

They were set down at the main entrance and it was evident how the great building had suffered. Gargoyles destroyed, statues defaced, walls partly demolished. But there was order, too, notice of times of masses and a crowd of people going in and out. They joined those going through the main doors. The grandeur of the place was impressive though there was still much evidence of destruction within it.

Catherine had noticed that a mass was about to begin.

'We should join the worshippers,' she said. 'We can blend in easily enough.'

It was true. There were all kinds of men and women milling

around and a variety of dress of both rich and poor. The three of them inserted themselves amongst an assorted group and bent their heads in prayer.

Will and Armstrong followed Catherine's lead and crossed themselves and genuflected at the appropriate times, but neither were taking notice of the priests at the high altar. Instead they whispered together, discussing what they might do if they had to evade any who pursued them. They were looking around the great building, eyes skinned, spotting potential hiding places and less obvious exits than the great front doors.

When the service finally came to an end Will took Catherine aside.

'I shall approach any person who looks official and ask after Father Jacques,' he said.

'Then I will do the same,' said Catherine.

'Have a story ready. And be careful who you approach.'

Catherine raised her eyebrows. 'Of course.'

While Will and Catherine dispersed, Armstrong wandered around the great building to inspect the places he'd noted where they might conceal themselves if necessary. But still he kept Will and Catherine in his sight.

Making enquiries was a wearisome business and Will and Catherine had to choose carefully who they spoke to. They did not want to raise any suspicions by seeming too anxious but both were conscious that it would not be long before de Menou's murder was discovered and the disappearance of Will, Armstrong and Catherine noted. Once Fouché was informed then nowhere would be safe.

They had to leave Paris at once, head for the coast and escape to England. Catherine could no longer be certain which of her agents were still undiscovered so it seemed that Jacques was their only hope.

As the day wore on, their frustration grew. Every now and again, Catherine and Will came together to confer but neither had gathered any information about Father Jacques or his whereabouts.

It was late afternoon and they were at a loss for what to do when Armstrong garnered the first clue. He had been lurking in dark corners, pretending deep piety if anyone approached him and murmuring prayers with closed eyes but not daring to speak should his accent give him away. It was in this position that he had overheard snatches of a conversation between two clerics.

'Forgive me mon Frere,' one was saying to the other, 'but I must take my leave. There are travellers at the guest house. They leave tomorrow and I must go and bid them farewell.'

At once, Armstrong was alert. He could hear no more of the conversation, but his eyes scanned the crowd, lessened now that mass was over, until he spotted Catherine. He wanted to run but did not want to draw attention to himself so he walked as fast as he could to where she stood, warming her hands at one of the great cast-iron stoves in the North aisle.

'It may be nothing,' he said breathlessly as he told her what he had heard and pointed over to where the man stood, already shrugging on his black clerical cloak and making to leave the building by a small door.

'We've had no other lead. Let's follow him,' she said.

'What of Fraser?'

'Will's eyes are on us,' said Catherine. 'He'll come.'

The two of them set off and Will, who was in a different part of the building, saw what they were doing and began to make his way over to them.

But at that moment, there was a commotion at the front of the cathedral and a large group of men crashed through the main entrance and ran inside shouting at the folk within to stay where they were.

'Stand still, everyone. Move at your peril.'

Will froze. Fouché's men.

He was already halfway across the floor of the cathedral heading for the place where he had seen the others but he could go no further for every person in the place had stopped in their tracks. There was a sudden eerie silence punctuated by some frightened whisperings.

The group of men were beginning to spread out now and search through the crowd.

And then Will saw him.

Fouché!

He was standing a little apart from the other searchers, his arms folded, his eyes darting this way and that.

Christ! I am trapped. De Menou's body has been discovered and his servants saw us leave. Fouché knows me by sight; he will have observed me when I waited at table and I warrant he never forgets a face.

Then a senior cleric was brought to Fouché and for a moment he was engaged in conversation with the man and they were both nodding their heads. The priest left Fouché and had obviously been given permission to speak to the clusters of frightened onlookers. As he approached a nearby group Will heard snatches of the conversation.

'A dreadful murder … the perpetrators were dropped off here at the cathedral … believed they may be hiding … must help bring them to justice.'

Fouché's been thorough, the bastard. He must have tracked down the driver of our fiacre.

Will kept his head lowered but he knew that it was only a matter of time before he was discovered.

Now Fouché was on the move again, systematically going to every group in turn, and he was not far away.

I might take out a few of them if I fought but there are twenty or thirty of them. And Fouché is inspecting every face. He will not miss me.

There was only one option.

Will turned his head very slowly. He was closest to the exit where he had seen the others leave; he knew there was a way out of the building there.

He edged into a space which gave him a clear run to the South aisle. The late afternoon darkness might give him some cover but they'd be after him the moment he made a move. He strained his eyes until he spotted the small door to the outside.

Then he took a deep breath and ran.

It happened so quickly that he was in the South aisle's shadows almost before Fouché and his men realised what had happened. A few precious moments and then a shout.

'After him! The villain went this way!' And the sound of pounding feet coming up behind him.

ROSEMARY HAYES

Will saw the small wooden door in front of him with a great iron key in the lock. He pulled open the door, wrenching the key out of the lock as he did so, and slipped outside. Behind him there were furious shouts, very close now. Will slammed the door shut and fumbled to lock it from the outside, cursing his clumsiness. Already someone was trying to open it from the inside and he pushed back against it with all his strength as he finally inserted the key. But it wasn't enough. There were too many of them. Then suddenly there was someone beside him, adding his weight to the door and finally Will managed to lock it.

'Christ sir, you took your bleeding time!'

'Duncan!'

'The lady's hiding nearby. We saw Fouché and his thugs arrive. We guessed you were trapped.'

'Where …' began Will.

'No time to explain. Reckon it'll take Fouché's men a while to run round here from the main door. We know where the guest house is. It's close by. Quick. Follow me.'

They ran. Armstrong was right. It was very close.

Catherine emerged from the shadows and joined them. No one spoke as they raced down a couple of streets and into a courtyard. Armstrong climbed the steps up to a solid house in the corner of the courtyard and pounded on the door.

'You'd better do the talking sir,' he said.

'Do we know if Jacques is there?'

'No idea.'

There was no response, and Armstrong banged on the door again. Then, at last, they heard the sound of approaching footsteps and the door opened. They did not wait to engage in polite conversation but the three of them pushed their way inside and banged the door shut behind them. A startled priest stared at them.

'My pardon, Father,' said Will, breathlessly. "I apologise for disturbing you. I am seeking my friend Father Jacques. He is recently come with some students from Granville. He told me that he would be staying at your guest house. I wonder if he is still here?'

The man continued to stare, open mouthed, looking Will up and down.

188

He sees a rough workman.

'Who is it that enquires?'

Will cleared his throat. 'My name is Etienne, sir. I am well acquainted with Father Jacques and would speak with him.' And then, when the man continued to frown at him, he went on. 'I must apologise for my rough apparel, but …'

Then Catherine joined the conversation and her appearance seemed to reassure the man. She smiled at him. 'It is a matter of some urgency, Father,' she said, putting a hand on his arm. 'Is Father Jacques here?'

Still he hesitated, then he backed down the passage. 'Wait here,' he said. 'I will make enquiries.'

They huddled inside the door.

'De Menou's body must have been discovered,' whispered Will.

Catherine nodded. 'We thought as much when we saw Fouché's men.'

'They'll know we can't be far away,' said Will. There will be a hue and cry.'

'Have courage,' said Catherine.

'He has no lack of that,' said Armstrong.

They waited in silence after that, Will pacing to and fro in the ill-lit passage.

'Will Fouché come here, do you suppose? To the guest house?'

'We must pray that he does not make the connection,' said Catherine. 'There is no reason why he should, after all.'

Then, after what seemed an interminable time, they heard the sound of footsteps and a tall figure came to a halt in front of them. The unmistakable figure of Father Jacques.

'Etienne!' he said, moving forward to shake Will's hand. 'And Pierre! What brings you here …' Then he saw Catherine.

'Blanche? My God, what …'

Catherine moved closer. 'Not Blanche, Jacques, but her sister, Catherine.'

Chapter Thirty-Three

For a moment, Jacques looked utterly perplexed.

'It is some time since we met, Jacques,' she said quietly. 'I have not visited my sister in a while.'

Jacques scratched his head. 'Of course, of course. Please forgive me. I was quite taken aback. You look so alike.'

Then he stood back. 'Come in, come in. I have been visited by another …'

As they went inside, Will asked. 'Another?'

'Another of your colleagues,' he replied. 'He, too, has sought me out. It seems he knows of my sympathies.'

Entering the priestly guesthouse, Will was immediately reminded of the time they had spent at Jacques' house near Granville. Of the quiet orderliness and tranquillity, of murmured voices and of robed men drifting hither and thither. For the first time in days, he felt some of the tension leave his body. Here, at least, he felt that they were among friends.

Yet who knows who are friends and who are foes?

Jacques took them into a small private room where a fire blazed in the grate and, standing with his back to the fire was a familiar figure.

Louis Bayard's head jerked up as they entered the room.

'Etienne! Pierre! What are you doing here? Have you come from de Menou's house? And who is your companion?'

Jacques answered him. 'This is Mademoiselle Catherine La Fargue,' he said. The sister of Madame Blanche de Valois. Blanche is a close neighbour of mine in Granville.'

Catherine cut in. 'There is no need for discretion here, Jacques,' she said. 'We all know that Blanche is your mistress.'

Momentarily, Jacques looked discomforted, then he shrugged and smiled.

Catherine continued. 'I know you operate independently, Jacques, but I am aware of your activities. You have done great work in helping those escaping the country and I thank you.'

'*You* thank me? I do not understand your involvement in this business.'

'Then,' said Catherine. 'Perhaps the moment has come for all to be revealed.'

Louis Bayard looked in puzzlement at Catherine, as did Jacques.

Catherine moved closer to Will and cleared her throat. Then, quietly and clearly, she revealed to the others that she was the mysterious Gaston and told them all that she had learnt while with de Menou and Fouché.

'Her bravery astonished me,' said Will.

She turned to him and smiled. 'But without your skill and bravery I would have been killed.'

Then it was Will's turn to tell Louis and Jacques of de Menou's murder and that that the three of them, he, Catherine and Armstrong were being pursued by Fouché.

There was much anxious whispered conversation then while Will, Armstrong and Catherine gave more details to the others. Then Will suddenly frowned and turned to Louis.

'And what of you, sir? We have put you in danger. No doubt suspicion will fall on you for having introduced myself and Pierre to de Menou's household.'

Louis stroked his chin. 'I doubt that, my friend. My charitable work is genuine. I find employment for returned soldiers and that is well known.' He grinned suddenly. 'I shall express horror that a couple of royalists have hoodwinked me.'

He turned to Catherine. 'We know, now, who Fouché suspects. He sent his men far and wide; all suspects' houses were visited last night but, thanks to your warning, none were caught.' He paused. 'However, it seems I am not under suspicion. My home was not visited nor was the restaurant.'

'I thank God for that,' she replied. 'Then you will stay here in Paris?'

'I have no intention to leave.'

'Then can I hand over responsibility for the Paris network to you?'

Louis bowed and nodded and Catherine continued. 'God willing I will make it safely to England and we shall inform Reeves of all that has happened. My sister and I have property in England and I shall live there for now.'

Jacques looked up sharply. 'Blanche has property in England?'

Catherine burst out laughing. 'My dear man, did you really not know that she was a royalist agent?'

'What! No, I had no idea. How …'

'By the saints, she's good at deception! And right under your nose. Did you never wonder at her long absences?'

'No. She has often travelled away since her widowhood, to Paris to see you, to visit other friends. I …'

Catherine looked round at the company. 'I suppose now I can reveal to you her part in our cause,' she said. 'Blanche, for some time, has travelled across to England disguised as a sailor, taking messages and gold to and fro and easing the passage of any royalist agents needing to escape or to be brought here from England. She used to operate out of Dieppe but has found Le Tréport less patrolled.' She smiled at Jacques' astonished expression. 'Those who know of her activities there call her Le Petit Matelot.'

Jacques continued to stare at Catherine. 'What a revelation,' he said. 'I know there was some gossip spread by her coachman about a lover further up the coast but I gave it no credence. I was sure she would not be faithless.'

'And you never questioned her?'

Jacques shook his head. 'Our time together was always so short.'

'And you had better ways of employing it, no doubt!'

Jacques coughed and changed the subject. 'But now, time is of the essence, is it not. It is obvious you cannot stay in Paris. How can I help?'

'By transporting us with all speed to Le Tréport,' said Catherine.'

Jacques frowned. 'But I am due to take some brethren back with me to Granville.'

Catherine put up her hand. 'Then make some excuse. They can stay here a few days longer, no doubt. This is more important. We must leave the country.' She gestured to Will and Armstrong. 'You say that Reeves will send a vessel to Le Tréport on the 14th? We must be there to board it.'

Chapter Thirty-Four

While Jacques and his fugitive passengers were making the journey West to the coast from Paris, Blanche was visiting her sailor friends in Le Tréport to make arrangements to gather in, hide and disguise the agents who had been unmasked. And her chandler colleague was busy relaying messages to safe houses along the route from Paris to alert them to be ready to receive an influx of fleeing royalists.

But they were not the only ones making arrangements.

After spying on Suzanne, the young man on horseback had urged his mount forward, conscious of the precious package in his saddlebag, and headed for the home of his handler a little further up the coast. Contrary to what he had told Suzanne, the mare he rode was fresh and eager, borrowed from his fellow spy, the groom at Father Jacques' house.

When the young man reached the home of his handler, he gave him the gold and the coded letter and explained how he had come by it.

His handler took the coded letter, frowning as he read it. 'Another new code,' he said. 'At least one I do not recognise.' He spat on the floor. 'These damned royalists are wily as foxes.' He turned to the young man: 'What of the girl who left it? Would she know how to decipher it? Should we bring her in?'

The young man looked shocked. 'She's an ignorant child, sir. She was simply doing her mistress's bidding.' He rubbed his sore leg. 'The groom at the stables assures me that if the lady does, indeed, support the royalist cause then none other knows of this.'

'Hmm,' said his handler. 'You say that the groom told you the lady is often away from home?'

'There's some rumour that she has a lover further up the coast.'

'More likely she is helping royalists escape.'

He picked up the package and weighed it in his hand. 'And no doubt these gold coins are destined for Paris to help the work of their spies.' He was silent for a while, then he looked at the young man before him.

'Napoleon is back in Paris,' he said slowly, not lowering his gaze.

The young man looked nonplussed. Then, suddenly, he caught his handler's drift.

'You don't think …?'

'When the Emperor is in Paris his life is always at risk. The Police Department will be redoubling their efforts to round up royalist spies and those that escape arrest will, no doubt, be coming West to the coast to escape to England, the rats.'

'Will they be heading to Dieppe, sir.'

'Dieppe or Le Tréport.'

'Should we alert the authorities, sir?'

'Indeed. And we should do it with all speed.'

'And what about the lady?'

'If she's not caught on the coast, she'll come home.' He smiled. 'And we have proof of her activities now. One way and another, she'll not escape.'

***

In Le Tréport, the royalist fugitives were arriving in small numbers, not in a crowd that might draw attention, for it was a small town. They went where they were directed, to the chandler's shop, to the cottages of fishing families or carpenters, to the homes of those who serviced the boats coming in and out of the port. Some were dressed in sailors' garb, some in workmen's clothes. They held their collective breath as the 14th approached and Le Petit Matelot went amongst them, discreetly giving them instructions, keeping them aware of activities, treading softly. She was among friends here and she knew who to trust. Usually she helped only a handful of those needing to leave the country but this time it was different and hiding so many in plain sight made her more than usually uneasy.

Father Jacques had driven his coach himself, trusting no one else with such a precious cargo. News would have spread of Catherine's disappearance and that of Will and Armstrong, so they had only stopped once, at a safe house known to Catherine, to change the exhausted horses. Then they continued on through the night, all acutely aware that three of them, at least, were being pursued by the law.

On the outskirts of Le Tréport, Jacques stopped the coach and his passengers alighted. He gave them his blessing, kissed Catherine's hand, then turned the horses and went back the way he had come. As he drove away, his heart was heavy as he thought about Blanche.

Will she be able to escape? Will the danger pass? Will she ever be able to return?

Catherine had changed into some rough peasant's clothes and Will and Armstrong were still in their workmen's garb, so they did not stand out as they walked down into the town, dwarfed by the great tall chalk cliffs. Catherine knew of Blanche's friend in the chandler's shop and when she entered it, Will and Armstrong stayed outside and waited until she emerged and hastily gave them instructions on where to go, each of them to a different hiding place. They were to keep indoors, only coming out when they were called for.

Officially, the jurisdiction of Fouché's secret police did not extend beyond Paris but local members of the National Guard had been told to be on the alert for escaping royalists. They had been instructed to keep a particular lookout for incoming vessels and some guards were keeping watch from the top of the cliffs. If they spotted any English vessels lurking outside the harbour, they were to act immediately. It was their reasoning that if there were fugitives hiding in the town, they would be rowed out to a vessel anchored there, possibly under cover of darkness, and then the guards would pounce, arresting not only the fugitives but also any helping them escape.

On the morning of the 14th, the signalman on top of the cliffs spied a ship heading for the harbour. He put his telescope to his eye.

'Vessel requesting entry to the harbour sir,' he said to the guard at his side. The man was instantly alert. 'One of ours?' he asked.

The signalman nodded. 'French signals, sir,' he said, 'Definitely one of ours.'

The man sighed. 'Give them permission then,' he said, and went back to the tedious business of keeping watch.

And so it was that *La Belle* slid into the harbour and tied up, in plain sight. The guard watched, yawning, as cargo was offloaded and outgoing cargo was reloaded. And if there seemed to be more sailors and navvies than usual around the harbour, rolling barrels and heaving boxes on and off, he did not note it. Nor did he note that one of the peasant women offering food to those on board, did not disembark.

Then all was quiet as the vessel bobbed in the water, lower now with the weight of her new cargo, waiting until the tide was right. Then the sails were hoisted, cracking as the wind filled them, and some of the crew helped speed her progress by taking to the oars as she made her way out into the Channel.

When they were well out to sea, Will went up on deck. Catherine and Blanche were there, standing close together by the rail, Catherine still wearing her stained and worn peasant's dress and Blanche still dressed as a sailor. They were silent, gazing back towards the French coast.

They turned as Will approached them.

'God knows when we shall see France again,' said Catherine. 'It may be a long time before it is safe for either of us to return.'

Will smiled down at them. 'You are the most resourceful women I have ever met,' he said. 'You will find a way.'

Chapter Thirty-Five

London

Will and Armstrong were in Westminster pacing up and down the lobby of the Alien Office, waiting to be called to the presence of John Reeves. They had been parted for a few days, Armstrong spending time with Sally and Will helping Catherine and Blanche settle in their temporary lodgings in London.

'This lobby is the coldest bleeding place in the city,' said Armstrong. 'Why does the man always keep us waiting?'

Will shrugged. 'Reeves is never one to hurry,' he said. He paused, frowning. 'Will you agree to another mission if he asks, Duncan?'

'I don't rightly know. Sal's got a notion of running a tavern together and I must say it has some appeal. What about you, sir? You got any plans.'

'For God's sake, stop calling me sir! Truly I don't know the answer to that.'

'That lovely Mademoiselle La Fargue in your plans?'

Will shook his head. 'I don't think so, Duncan. She's high born and I am not. And what could I offer her? I'm still a disgraced soldier with no pension.'

'But you have a job.'

'Aye. And it's a mighty dangerous one.'

'As is hers.'

Their conversation was cut short when a servant came to fetch them and they were taken up to Reeves' chamber.

Will looked about him at the familiar room with its gleaming furniture, the turkey rug on the floor, the decanter of fine wine on the side table and the roaring fire in the grate. When he had first met Reeves, he had been not a little over-awed by the man but over time, awe had turned to respect and even fondness.

John Reeves rose to greet them.

'A successful mission I hear,' he said, shaking Will's hand and patting Armstrong on the shoulder.

Will raised his eyebrows. Reeves was always one step ahead of them and had already been to visit Blanche and Catherine.

'Partly successful, I would say, sir.'

'And I would say it was wholly successful. De Menou has been dispatched, Gaston has been rescued and there is a new and unsuspected head of the Paris network who will go about rebuilding it.'

'The plot to assassinate the Emperor had to be abandoned.'

'That was nothing to do with you.'

Then followed one of Reeves' long silences as he picked up his silver snuff box, opened it slowly, took out a pinch of snuff and put it on the back of his hand and sniffed it up his right nostril. Then, with great deliberation, he did the same again but sniffed it up the left nostril.

'Now gentlemen,' he said. 'Let us sit down together and drink a glass of my excellent fortified wine while you tell me every detail of your adventures in France.'

It was a long meeting. Reeves questioned them on every aspect, on who had been exposed, who was unsuspected, any knowledge of new safe houses, of ones that had been discovered and of the extent of Fouché's influence in Paris.

When they had finished, he sat, deep in thought, his fingers steepled under his chin. Then he smiled at them, his hawkish features suddenly transformed.

'So, your faces are known in Paris now – and elsewhere no doubt,' he said. 'Perhaps it would be wise not to step on French soil again for some time. Fouché is a cruel man and he likes to crush his enemies, particularly those who have outwitted him.'

'Very well, sir,' said Will.

'With pleasure, sir,' said Armstrong. 'I've had my fill of sea travel.'

Reeves rose, indicating that their meeting was at an end. 'There will be other missions,' he said. 'I shall have more work for you and when I need you, I shall call on your services, you can be sure of that.'

Out on the street, Armstrong let out his breath. 'Sounds like we're on leave then, sir. Fancy coming with me to see Sal and

Lottie?'

'Not just now, Duncan. I have another visit to make.'

Armstrong rubbed the side of his nose and winked. 'Off to see the lovely French lady are you?'

Will shook his head.

Armstrong raised an eyebrow. 'No future there?'

'I think not.'

Armstrong frowned. 'You know, sir,' he said, his face serious. 'That business in Portugal … the lady there.'

Will turned on him. 'I told you never to mention that. The matter is closed.'

But Armstrong persisted. 'It's not, sir,' he said quietly. 'There's unresolved business there. You spared her reputation and sacrificed your own. I saw how you were together. I …'

'Enough!' The expression on Will's face was set.

'Have it you own way,' muttered Armstrong. Then he raised a hand in farewell and strode off in the direction of Drury Lane.

Will stood where he was for a few moments longer, his emotions conflicted. Armstrong had opened a festering wound, a wound he'd persuaded himself had healed.

In his heart, though, he knew that it had not. It would never heal.

He sighed and straightened his shoulders. He could not allow himself to dwell on what might have been. He must forget all that. He had a new life now.

On these London streets, though, the memories of Jack were close and with them an overwhelming feeling of guilt.

He turned and started walking away slowly. Not towards Catherine La Fargue's lodgings but in the opposite direction.

Towards Lincoln's Inn.

To Clara.

ROSEMARY HAYES

Historical Note

In this second story in the 'Soldier Spy' trilogy, some of the
characters are real, others entirely fictional. John Reeves was real.
He was head of the Alien Office from 1803-1814 and had a
network of agents who sent information back to their handlers.
Messages were often written in code and/or in special inks to try
and ensure that their contents would not be revealed should they
be intercepted. Each intelligence agency had its own ciphers and
ink composition.

Joseph Fouché, The Minister of Police was real. He began his
career as a maths teacher and evolved into a moderate and then
radical legislator. He cultivated every political movement of the
day. After preaching clemency for Louis XVI, Fouché voted to
send the King to the guillotine. After writing "The first Communist
Manifesto of Modern Times" he became a multi-millionaire. He
led the brutal repression of an anti-revolutionary movement,
earning him the nickname 'The Butcher of Lyon'. After serving
Robespierre, Fouché engineered his overthrow and rose to
Minister of Police under the Directory, which he then helped to
overthrow before putting his network of informants in Napoleon's
service. After turning against the Emperor, Fouché served the new
King Louis XVIII – whose brother he had helped send to the
guillotine. Thus, Fouché served the Revolution, the Directory, the
First Empire and the Restoration. His face was said to resemble a
weasel – and his less flattering portraits bear this out!

'Le Petit Matelot' did exist (though I have changed the dates
when she was active to suit the story). Her real name was Arabella
Williams, originally from Liverpool. Her handler was William
Wickham and she became known as *'le petit matelot'* – the little
sailor – as she had acted as a courier passing papers between
France and England for a number of years disguised as a sailor,
without being caught. One of her contacts in France was a royalist
by the name of Louis Bayard (who also appears in the story) whose
mistress ran a restaurant in Paris which served as a safe meeting
place and shelter for the agents.

200

THE KING'S AGENT

Arabella had her own property in France where she had lived for some years, which she also used as a safe house for other agents as and when required. Another of her contacts was Abbé Ratel.

The character of Father Jacques is based very loosely on that of Abbé Ratel who, earlier in the war, organised a network of royalists to keep watch around the port of Boulogne and provide early warning of any invasion. Reports were sent to England through fishermen recruited by Ratel – who was reputed to have a very beautiful mistress.

Many Jersey fishermen were royalist agents, one making almost 200 trips over to France; he was eventually unmasked and executed. Although I do not know his name, he appears as Gabriel in the story.

Pipette was also a real person, a fisherman's wife and royalist agent. And young women were often disguised as young men to confuse their pursuers.

There were several attempts to assassinate Napoleon, the most famous being in Paris on the evening of December 24th 1800. Almost certainly funded by the British, this very nearly succeeded when a cart exploded just after Napoleon's carriage had passed, killing bystanders.

Malmaison, Empress Josephine's country chateau, was the site of others, including the poisoned snuff put into a replica of Napoleon's snuff box and placed on his desk there.

There was a galley which was intercepted just off the French port of Gravelines and this appears in the first 'Soldier Spy' story. At the time she was called *The Apus of London* but it is likely her name was often changed to suit her mission. She makes an appearance here as *La Belle*.

During the 'dechristianisation' of France at the time of the Revolution, churches were closed or used for other purposes. Their treasures were stolen and their buildings severely damaged. Notre Dame did not escape this vandalism. Many of its statues were destroyed, its fittings and fixtures plundered and the building fell into a period of decay and neglect.

Priests and nuns suffered terribly during the French Revolution (1789-1799) and many were murdered.

ROSEMARY HAYES

About the Author

After a career as a writer of children's and young adult fiction, Rosemary Hayes has recently started writing historical fiction for adults. Her first book in the genre was *The King's Command,* also published by Sharpe Books, about the terror and tragedy suffered by the French Huguenots during the reign of Louis XIV. Based loosely on the experience of her own Huguenot ancestors, it is a fast-moving story of love and loss. It traces the gradual disintegration of a family who refused to convert to Catholicism, their persecution, their courage and their eventual flight to England in the late 17th century. The book has already collected a couple of awards and some outstanding reviews.

Soldier Spy: Traitor's Game is the first book in a trilogy set during the time of the Napoleonic Wars. The main protagonist is Captain Will Fraser, a disgraced and penniless ex-soldier, the victim of a conspiracy led by a jealous and influential officer. Falsely accused of insubordination and cowardice and dismissed from his regiment, Will is desperate to clear his name. But then his life takes an unexpected turn and he and his injured friend, Sergeant Duncan Armstrong, inadvertently become embroiled in the murky world of spying.

In this second book in the trilogy, *The King's Agent,* Will and Armstrong, now officially the King's agents, are sent on an urgent mission to France. For Will, it is a mission of revenge.

Rosemary's many books for children are written in a variety of different genres, from edgy teenage fiction (*The Mark),* historical fiction (*The Blue Eyed Aborigine* and *Forgotten Footprints),* middle grade fantasy (*Loose Connections, The Stonekeeper's Child* and *Break Out)* to chapter books for early readers and texts for picture books. Many of her books for young people have won or been shortlisted for awards and several have been translated into different languages.

Rosemary has travelled widely but now lives in South Cambridgeshire. She has a background in publishing, having worked for Cambridge University Press before setting up her own company Anglia Young Books which she ran for some years. She has been a reader for a well known authors' advisory service and runs creative writing workshops for both children and adults.

Visit her website at www.rosemaryhayes.co.uk
Find her on **X** (formerlyTwitter) @HayesRosemary

Printed in Dunstable, United Kingdom